The Haunting
of Gull Cottage

Kezzie stopped dead.

A woman stood on the bridge. A youngish woman with long dark hair, staring at the house. A woman who appeared to have no legs, just her head and body floating above the ground…

Kezzie felt paralysed, unable even to breathe. Then, slowly, the woman turned to look straight at her. Her eyes were dark and very sad. She raised a hand as if in greeting and started to glide across the bridge.

Hippo Ghost

The Haunting of Gull Cottage

Tessa Krailing

Hippo

Scholastic Children's Books
Commonwealth House, 1–19 New Oxford Street,
London WC1A 1NU, UK
a division of Scholastic Ltd
London ~ New York ~ Toronto ~ Sydney ~ Auckland

First published by Scholastic Ltd, 1996

ISBN 0 590 13432 9

Typeset by TW Typesetting, Midsomer Norton, Avon
Printed by Cox & Wyman Ltd, Reading, Berks
10 9 8 7 6 5 4 3 2 1

Contents

Chapter 1
Holiday Let

Gull Cottage stood alone on the river bank, surrounded by tall elms. It looked harmless enough with its green front door and square-paned windows, yet for years it had remained empty. Nobody wanted to live in it because it had a bad reputation. Haunted, the locals said. Not surprising, considering what happened there in the past...

The woman leaned over the grey stone wall, staring at the cottage – *her* cottage, legally, because it stood on her land. For two years she had been trying to sell the place, without success. There was only one alternative to selling and that was to turn it into a holiday let. Smarten it up a bit, equip it with china and cutlery, and put an advertisement in the national press:

"Cottage to let on Isle of Wight, sleeps six, quiet location on river creek, ideal family holiday."

She smiled to herself. Yes, that was the answer. Let it to strangers who knew nothing of its history. A few noisy children running around might banish the ghosts once and for all. Her mind made up, she turned away, calling to her dog. "Jasper! Jasper, where are you?"

The black labrador was waiting for her on the other side of the river. Usually so brave, he would never cross the narrow stone bridge that connected the cottage with the road. But of course animals know instinctively when there's something wrong with a place. The woman hoped that if a family did come here for a holiday they wouldn't bring a dog with them. She might even put that in the advertisement. *"Sorry, no dogs."*

She hurried back across the bridge,

shivering in the strange, misty chill that always seemed to hang above the water.

James wasn't keen on the idea when his father first suggested it.

"Easter's a funny time of year to go to the seaside," he said. "We shan't be able to swim or play on the beach."

"Don't be so sure," said Dad. "The weather can be quite warm in April. Besides, it's cheaper to go away out of season – and places are a lot less crowded than they are in the summer."

In the good old days, James thought, when there was just the four of them – Dad, Mum, himself and his sister Alison – they had always gone away in the summer, usually to Wales or Cornwall and once even for a camping holiday in France. But now there were seven of them – *seven* – and camping was out of the question because of the Squaller.

"Hotels aren't usually keen on taking families with a baby," he pointed out. "Especially one as noisy as ours."

Dad raised his eyebrows. "Who said anything about a hotel? I was thinking of a country cottage, preferably miles away from anywhere so you kids can make as much row as you like without upsetting anyone."

"A country cottage? I thought you said the seaside."

"Both," Dad said triumphantly. "Here, take a look at this."

He spread a newspaper over the kitchen table, opened it at the holiday page and jabbed his finger at a short paragraph beginning "*Cottage to let…*"

James read it, twice. "It says 'river creek'. That's not the seaside."

"The Isle of Wight's only eleven miles wide. You're never far from the sea, wherever you go. And it says '*quiet location, ideal family holiday*'."

"It also says '*no dogs*'."

"We haven't got a dog, so that's no problem. Anyway I've already telephoned the owner and she says we can have it if we want. It's at a place called Jacob's Creek on the north side

4

of the island."

"What does Mum think?" James asked.

"I haven't told her yet." He folded the newspaper up again. "But she'll love the idea, I know she will."

Good old Dad, always the optimist, certain he could get everyone to see things his way. Three years ago, when one of his workmates had told him that he and his wife were fostering a couple of kids whose mother couldn't look after them any more, Dad had been so impressed that he suggested to Mum they should do the same thing. "How about it, Jan? We've got plenty of room and you're great with kids, you know you are. I reckon we're just the kind of people they're looking for."

And that was how the fostering business had started. In the past three years a variety of children had come and gone, all ages, shapes and sizes. At present there were just three of them – Kezzie, Baz and the Squaller. Baz was OK, too quiet to be any trouble, and even the Squaller wasn't a major problem, apart from keeping everyone awake at night. But Kezzie…

Kezzie was a real pain in the neck, in James's opinion. The thought of going on holiday with her filled him with dismay. He read the advertisement for a third time, hoping to find a snag. "It says the cottage sleeps six," he said, "and we're seven."

"Six and a baby," said Dad. "I told the woman and she said she could easily provide a cot for the Squaller."

Mum came into the kitchen just in time to hear this last remark. "I do wish you'd stop calling him that," she said, drawing the shawl tighter around the baby in her arms as if to protect him. "Poor little mite, he only cries because he's under-nourished. As soon as we've got him up to his proper weight he'll be good as gold." She sat on the nearest chair and reached for the feeding bottle.

James glanced doubtfully at the baby's wizened face. It was Kezzie who had christened him the Squaller. The name given to him by the nurses at the premature baby unit was Brandon, because he was found in a cardboard box on the steps of St Brandon's Church. He was the youngest child Mum and Dad had ever fostered and by far the noisiest. The only time he was quiet was when he had the feeding bottle stuck in his mouth. Like now.

"Better call the others," said Mum, "or they'll be late for school."

Baz and Alison came into the kitchen together. They were about the same age, although no one would guess it by looking at them. Baz was on the small side for ten, very dark and quiet, whereas Alison was plump and red-haired and bouncy. She went straight over to the baby and started making "goo goo" noises. "Can I hold him, Mum? Can I give him his bottle?"

"Best leave him where he is." Mum glanced at her watch. "Where's Kezzie?"

"Still asleep," said Alison.

"James, go and give her a yell."

He pulled a face. "Oh Mum, must I?"

"Yes – and don't give up until she answers."

He went to the foot of the stairs and yelled. No answer. He climbed halfway and yelled again. Still no answer. He thundered up to the landing and hammered on her door. "Kezzie? Kezzie, you up yet?"

A faint groan came from the bedroom Kezzie shared with Alison.

"Did you hear me? Are you awake?"

"Shove off," said a muffled voice.

"Mum says you've got to come down for breakfast."

"Not hungry."

"You will be if you don't eat anything."

"Get lost, Jamie."

James gave up in disgust. He hated being called Jamie. It made him feel like an infant. That was the trouble with Kezzie. At thirteen she was a year older than he was and never let him forget it. Until six months ago, when she came to live with them, he had been the oldest and he strongly resented being bossed about by a complete stranger, especially a girl.

Mum looked up as he entered the kitchen. "Is she coming?"

He shook his head, sat down at the table and poured some cornflakes into a bowl.

Mum sighed. "Oh well, I expect she'll snatch a piece of toast on her way out. I've enough to do without chasing after Kezzie."

"Quite right," Dad agreed. "You know what you need, Jan? A holiday!" With a flourish he opened the newspaper and showed her the advertisement.

"Oh, yes?" Mum raised a sceptical eyebrow. "A fine holiday that'd be, stuck right out in the country and me trying to cook meals on a strange stove. Thanks a bunch, Rob!"

"The kids will help you. Kezzie can do some of the cooking."

"Kezzie? If it was left to her we'd starve."

"I'll do it," said Alison. "I can cook."

"Boiled eggs and chocolate fudge," said Mum. "We can't live on that for a week. Anyway, we can't afford a holiday."

"We can afford this one," said Dad. "The cottage is going really cheap. If I hadn't booked it straight away somebody else would soon snap it up."

Mum stared at him. "You've already booked it?"

"Too good an opportunity to miss – and the woman who owns it seemed really keen we should take the place."

"Must be something wrong with it," muttered James.

"What's the matter with you all? Here I am, offering you the chance of a lifetime, and you all sit there looking as if you'd been insulted. Do you want a holiday by the seaside or not?"

There was a pause. Then everyone started saying things like, "Well, OK. Might be fun. Better than staying at home." And before long they were beginning to sound quite enthusiastic.

Except Baz, who sat looking as if the bottom had dropped out of his world.

Chapter 2
Jacob's Creek

Kezzie hated the journey to the Isle of Wight. First they had to drive down to Portsmouth and it was a horrible squash on the back seat of the Tolliver's old estate waggon. Jan Tolliver took up a lot of space because she was nursing the Squaller, and Kezzie was sandwiched between Baz and Alison, while James sat in the front beside his father so that he could navigate.

Kezzie scowled at the back of James's neck. Why couldn't it be her in front beside the driver? She could navigate every bit as efficiently as James. But no, she – Kezia MacBride, thirteen years old and well used to

11

taking care of herself – was stuck in the back with the young ones. As usual.

She hadn't wanted to come on this holiday anyway. They'd fixed it up one morning at breakfast while she was still in bed. "Guess what, we're going to the Isle of Wight!" they had told her, as if it were the greatest treat in the world. "I'm too old for seaside holidays," she had protested. But they had only laughed and said she'd enjoy it.

At last they reached Portsmouth and drove on to the ferry. As soon as they had parked on the car deck they got out and climbed the stairs to an enormous lounge surrounded by plate glass windows. James immediately set off with his father to fetch some drinks from the buffet bar. Alison disappeared to the lavatory. By the time they returned the ferry had left the harbour and was chugging steadily across the waters of the Solent.

"You can see the Island already." Jan pointed to a low, humped shape on the horizon, like a sleeping elephant. "We should be there in about thirty minutes."

Kezzie noticed that Baz's face had gone an odd greenish colour. "Are you feeling seasick?" she asked.

Before Baz could answer James said, "Don't be silly, Kez. He can't possibly get seasick on a short trip like this. Besides, it's dead calm."

Kezzie glared at him. "You can get seasick on a duckpond if you're that way inclined. Come on, Baz. Let's go and get some fresh air."

Baz followed her obediently to the exit.

It was cold on deck, with a stiff breeze coming off the sea. They found a sheltered spot and stood huddled in their anoraks, watching the churning wake of the ferry as it drew farther and farther away from the mainland. Kezzie's spirits lifted in spite of herself. It was a sort of adventure to be leaving England, almost like going abroad.

"Feeling better?" she asked Baz.

He shook his head.

Kezzie sighed. In an odd sort of way she felt responsible for him, perhaps because he was an outsider like herself and had lived most of his life in children's homes, also like herself. She asked, "OK, so what's wrong?"

"I hate going to strange places. Anything can happen. They make me scared." His lower lip began to quiver.

"It's only for a week!" Impatiently Kezzie fished a tissue out of her pocket and gave it to him. "Nothing much can happen in a week. You'll be quite safe, I promise."

He blew his nose and handed her back the handkerchief.

But an hour later, as they drove down the narrow, bumpy road leading to Jacob's Creek, she found herself sharing Baz's unease. This was the most unsafe-looking place she had ever seen. Kezzie was a city girl, born and bred. She liked bright lights, crowded shops and pavements beneath her feet – not this flat, deserted marshland with its spiky hedgerows and bare black trees. Some holiday this was going to be!

Rob Tolliver stopped the car beside a bridge leading to a small stone house. "I think that must be it," he said. "The letter said we had to cross a river. Yes, it's got the name over the door – Gull Cottage."

"There's a black dog sitting in the middle of the road," said Alison. "It looks as if it's waiting for someone."

"Probably Mrs Dent, the owner," said her father. "I told her which ferry we were catching and she said she'd be here to give us the keys." He tooted at the dog to make it get out of the way.

As they drove over the narrow bridge Kezzie shivered. She peered out at the house with its grey stone walls and blank windows. It looked pretty decrepit, she thought, even though someone had recently given the front door a lick of green paint. Must be a hundred years old at least.

They all got out and stretched their legs. The cottage had no garden, just a dirt yard leading up to the front door. A row of bored-looking gulls perched on top of its slate roof and beyond it, in the distance, lay the flat grey waters of the creek.

"I know the advertisement said it was a

15

quiet location," Jan Tolliver remarked, "but I didn't expect it to be as quiet as this. There isn't another house in sight."

"Perfect," said Rob with a pleased grin.

At that moment the front door opened and a woman came out to meet them, smiling brightly.

"You must be the Tollivers. I can't tell you how pleased I am to see you!" She sounded quite gushy, Kezzie thought, almost as if she were nervous about something. "My, what a lot of children you've got. I hope they're going to make plenty of noise."

"I can guarantee that," said Rob, and as if on cue the Squaller opened his mouth and began to cry.

"He's hungry," said Jan. "We'd better get unpacked as soon as possible."

"I'll help," said Kezzie.

"No, I'll do it," James said at once. "I'm the strongest."

Kezzie snorted. "You – strong? You've got muscles like a jellyfish!"

"Yours are more like cockles. I don't know

how—"

"OK, that's enough," Rob said quickly. "James will help me unpack. Kezzie, you take the younger ones off to explore."

"Not too far," warned Jan. "And don't go near the water."

They disappeared into the cottage with Mrs Dent, leaving Kezzie with Baz and Alison. "I wonder why she hopes we'll make plenty of noise?" Alison said, looking puzzled. "People usually hope exactly the opposite."

"I expect she's mad," Kezzie said. "She must be, to live in a place like this."

It really got her goat, the way Rob and Jan always lumped her with the younger kids. In some ways they were the best foster-parents she'd had so far. They weren't over-fussy or over-strict, and had never asked her to call them Mum or Dad or anything soft like that but suggested she used their Christian names. It was only this stupid business of treating James as if he were the oldest that annoyed her. *James will help me unpack.* She was as strong as James any day. Stronger.

Alison walked to the middle of the bridge and stood looking down into the water. "It's like being in a castle with a moat," she said. "I've never lived this close to a river before."

"You call this a river?" Kezzie said contemptuously, going to join her. "I'd call it a pathetic little stream."

Baz followed. "I can't see any fish," he said, peering over the low stone wall.

"Neither can I." Alison shivered. "Isn't it cold here? Much colder than at home."

Baz said uneasily, "I don't like it. I think it's spooky."

"Now don't start imagining things," Kezzie warned him. "You'll only frighten yourself."

She knelt on the wall and leaned over, wondering how deep it was. The water was grey, almost silvery, and just below the surface lay a face, pale and moon-like, gazing up at her, the mouth an open O. Startled, she drew back, then told herself not to be stupid, it was only her own reflection. She leaned over again, as far as she could...

"Careful or you'll fall in," warned Alison.

But Kezzie didn't even hear her. She was too busy staring down at the face. It looked so strange, not a bit recognizable as her own. She pulled down the corners of her mouth to see if her reflection did the same, but the face in the water stayed fixed in a strange grimace as if silently screaming. A wave of clammy fear swept over Kezzie. She wanted to look away but couldn't. It was as if the face was trying to tell her something, almost as if it was pleading for help. Fascinated, she bent even closer, but at that moment a chill little wind blew up, rippling the water, and the image was lost. Kezzie stood up, her knees shaking.

"I'm going to talk to that dog," said Baz.

"What dog?" Kezzie tried to pull herself together.

"The black one sitting in the middle of the road. He must belong to Mrs Dent."

"Well OK, but be careful," warned Kezzie, who had once been chased by a large black labrador.

Baz walked straight up to the dog, holding out his hand, and within minutes was crouched down beside him, patting his head. "It's OK," he called out. "He's friendly." But when he tried to coax the dog to follow him back across the bridge it refused to come.

"Oh, leave him be," said Kezzie. She turned back to the cottage, impatient to get indoors where it would be safe.

As they reached the front door Mrs Dent appeared, still smiling her bright, nervous smile. "Back already? You didn't go far."

"There's a dog waiting in the road," Alison told her. "Does he belong to you?"

"You mean Jasper. Yes, he's mine." She had small brown eyes that darted about all over the place – everywhere, Kezzie noticed, except at the person she was speaking to.

"But we couldn't make him come over the bridge," said Baz.

"No, well … he knows he's not allowed inside the cottage," said Mrs Dent. "I don't want him messing up the floor with his muddy paws."

"Is that why you put 'no dogs' in the advertisement?" Alison asked.

"Exactly!" Mrs Dent beamed at her as if she had said something really intelligent. "Now I must go. Enjoy your holiday." She hurried across the bridge and called to her dog.

"She *is* mad," said Kezzie, gazing after her. "If it's mud she's worried about why let the cottage to a load of kids?"

"Never mind her," said Alison. "Let's go and see what our bedrooms are like."

It was dark inside the cottage. The surrounding elm trees shut out most of the light and the windows had small leaded panes. On the ground floor there was a small living room with a wood-burning stove, a large kitchen and a cloakroom leading into the bathroom.

"I hadn't realized the bathroom was downstairs," Jan said. "That's going to be a nuisance if anyone needs to go to the lavatory during the night."

"We'll be glad of that stove in the evenings, though," Rob said. "There's a good supply of logs in the basket and Mrs Dent says that if we need more we can collect them from the farm."

"Fine," said Jan. "As long as it's not me that has to clean the grate."

Upstairs there were three bedrooms, a large one with a cot installed and two others. The smallest of these had bunk beds. They tossed for it and to Kezzie's annoyance she and Alison won. She hated bunk beds. They tossed again and she drew the bottom bunk. Even worse. Now she would have to lie and listen to Alison tossing and turning above her. Alison was a restless sleeper and sometimes snored.

That first night in the cottage she lay awake for hours. There was something missing but at first she couldn't work out what it was. Then she realized that at home – the Tollivers' home, that is – there was always the sound of distant traffic. It went on all night, a steady comforting rumble. But here there was nothing, just an empty silence.

Except that when she listened properly it wasn't silence, because outside she could hear the sound of running water. That must be the river. It made her think of the bridge, and of the strange reflection she had seen when she had looked into the water, that face staring up at her with the round dark O where the mouth should be...

With a groan she pulled up the bedclothes to shut out the menacing dark.

Chapter 3
Grockles and Ghosts

Next morning James awoke feeling more cheerful. Last night he'd had serious misgivings about Gull Cottage. The chimney smoked, the living room seemed cramped with six people and a baby in it, and worst of all the television didn't work properly. Trying to watch his favourite soap on a flickering screen with the Squaller yelling in the background had been a nightmare.

But this morning, with the sun shining through the curtains on to the striped quilt, it didn't seem so bad. He leaped out of bed and dressed quickly. Baz was still asleep, curled up in a ball with a pillow over his head. He often slept like that. It was a wonder he didn't suffocate.

There was no sound from the girls' room as he crept downstairs, but when he reached the kitchen he found his mother already seated at the table in her dressing-gown, feeding the Squaller. "Hello," he said. "I thought I was the first."

"Not quite." She glanced at his sweatshirt and jeans. "I see you're dressed, but I didn't hear you go to the bathroom?"

"No. Well, I couldn't, could I? There isn't one upstairs." He started opening cupboards, looking for the variety packs of cereal they had brought with them.

"There's one down here, though. Go and wash before you eat."

Sighing, he obeyed her. By the time he returned she had put the Squaller down in his carry-cot and poured herself a mug of tea. "How did you sleep?" she asked him.

"Not bad. I did hear the Squa – er, the baby crying once, but it seemed to be coming from a long way off. I suppose that's because the walls are so thick."

She handed him a glass of orange juice. "James, sit down. I want to talk to you."

His heart sank. He could tell from her voice that he was about to receive a parental lecture. There had been quite a few of those since they started fostering. He pulled out a chair and sat down.

"I hope you realize," she began, "that this is the first proper holiday Kezzie and Baz have ever had in their lives? We've got to do our best to make it a happy time for them – and that means not so much arguing and squabbling over petty trifles."

"You're talking about me and Kezzie," he said.

"Yes, I am. Please try to get on with her, James."

"She's so bossy!"

"Yes, but so are you. The trouble is you both want to be top dog and you can't be, not all the time. You've got to give and take a little." She smiled at him. "I'd like this holiday to be the time when we really start behaving like a family. I want to see Baz come out of his shell and Kezzie stop looking as if she wants to pick a fight with everyone. Please, James. It's important to me."

"OK," he said with a sigh. "I'll do my best."

"Thanks." She turned as Alison entered the kitchen, followed by Dad. "Goodness, you're early. I thought you'd all have a lie-in seeing it's the first day."

"I needed to go to the bathroom," said Alison, beating her father to it by a short head.

Soon afterwards Baz came down and even Kezzie appeared before the end of the meal, looking pale and subdued. If only she was always like this, James thought, it wouldn't be so hard to get along with her.

While they ate they discussed their plans for the day. "My first job will be cleaning the grate," Dad said, "and then I ought to go shopping. Even though we've brought the basic essentials we could do with some fresh vegetables and fruit. James, do you want to come with me?"

Before he could answer Mum said, "Why don't you take Kezzie? She knows what we need. Kezzie, you'd like a trip into the town, wouldn't you?"

"The town?" Kezzie brightened. "Yeah, I'll go."

"What about the rest of us?" Alison demanded. "What are *we* going to do?"

"Explore," said James.

"Good idea," said his father. "Mrs Dent gave me a map of this area yesterday. I'll find it for you."

When they had cleared away the breakfast things James spread the map over the kitchen table. "The creek's basically a Y-shape," he said. "There's the harbour mouth, and then the river divides into two. On one side it turns into a sort of lake and on the other, where we are, it goes quite a long way inland."

"Where's our cottage?" asked Alison, kneeling on a chair beside him.

"About here, I should think. Yes, look – it's

marked. Gull Cottage. All this area on the right of the harbour seems to be some sort of nature reserve…"

"And that must be the farm where Mrs Dent lives!"

James folded the map. "We'll take this with us. Baz, do you want to come?"

Baz nodded uncertainly.

"You'd better wear wellingtons," said Mum. "Mrs Dent warned me there are salt-marshes between here and the sea and they can be pretty muddy. Dangerous too, so take care where you put your feet."

"We will," James promised. "Come on, Ally. Baz."

Outside the cottage they stopped, taking stock of their surroundings. It was a crisp, clear morning with hardly any wind. On the other side of the river the ground rose up, thickly forested, towards a line of distant hills. There was no sound except the flurry of a moorhen emerging from the reeds, followed by a flotilla of chicks.

"It's very peaceful here," Alison said. "Do

you like it, Baz?"

"It's OK," Baz muttered, but he still looked uncertain.

"If we turn left across the bridge we'll be going upriver," James said. "If we turn right we should come to the harbour."

"Let's go right. I want to see the sea." Alison set off, her pony-tail bouncing against her anorak.

They crossed the bridge and followed the road until eventually it brought them to the river mouth. Here there was a definite tang of salt, gulls riding the air currents where the river met the sea, and a cluster of boats moored near a building marked Sadler's Boatyard. While Alison and Baz went to watch a pair of swans foraging near the slip-way, James stopped to look over the boatyard wall.

He saw a man working on the hull of a yacht suspended in a cradle. "Good morning," said James.

The man glanced up. He was young, with fair curly hair and the shiny, reddened skin of someone who spends most of his time out-of-doors. "Morning," he said in a friendly tone, and went back to his work.

"I was wondering," James said, "if you ever hire out boats for fishing?"

The young man straightened. "We do," he said cautiously. "But not to kids."

"It's for my dad as well."

"That's different." He came closer to the wall. "Here on holiday, are you?"

James nodded. "We're staying at Gull Cottage."

The young man stared at him. "Did you say … Gull Cottage?"

"Yes, we arrived yesterday."

At that moment another, older man appeared in the doorway. He called out, "Dave! That was Sam Hurst on the phone wanting to know if his boat's ready. You anywhere near finished yet?"

"Not quite. Dad, come over here. You'll never believe this. Mary Dent's gone and let Gull Cottage to some grockles. This kid's one of them."

The man came to join them. James could

see the family likeness: his face was even ruddier than his son's. But what on earth was a grockle?

"Well, well," said the older man, shaking his head in wonder. "And what's your name, young fellow?"

"James. James Tolliver. That's my sister Alison over there and – well, Baz is sort of my brother." Too difficult to explain why they were such a complicated family.

"Nice to meet you, James. I'm Joe Sadler and this here's my son Dave. How long are you staying at Gull Cottage?"

"A week." Curiosity overcame him. "What's wrong with it?"

"Nothing," said Joe Sadler, a little too quickly. "Nothing at all."

"Except it's haunted," Dave said with a grin.

"Now Dave," said his father, "there's no need to go scaring the lad. That's just an old superstition, on account of its history."

"What history?" asked James.

Dave shrugged. "Someone got killed there – oh, about two hundred years ago. There's said to be a ghost, but … well, Dad's right. It's only superstition. You don't want to worry about it."

"I've never seen a ghost round there and I don't know anyone who has," Joe Sadler said. "Dave, I told Sam Hurst his boat would be ready by lunchtime so you'd better get a move on."

When he'd gone James asked, "What's a grockle?"

Dave chuckled. "You are. It means a visitor from the mainland, someone who's here on holiday. You're a grockle and I'm a caulkhead, because I live here. That's c-a-u-l-k, by the way, not the cork of a bottle. It's the stuff we use to stop up the seams of a boat so the water doesn't get in – which is the job I'm supposed to be doing right now." He turned back to the yacht in the cradle, then called over his shoulder, "Come and see us when you and your dad want to hire a boat."

"Thanks, we will," said James. Thoughtfully he made his way down to the slipway to join the others.

"These swans are ever so fierce," said Alison. "One of them just chased Baz up the bank."

"I expect they're hungry," said James. "Next time we come we'll bring them some bread."

As they walked back to the cottage he nearly told them what he had learned at the boatyard, but on second thoughts he decided to keep it to himself. Baz was nervous enough without being told that Gull Cottage was supposed to be haunted.

Anyway, it was only a story. An old superstition, Joe Sadler had called it. Not worth repeating.

Chapter 4
Something in the Atmosphere

Kezzie enjoyed her trip to Newport. It was great to be in a town again, with shops and traffic and solid pavement beneath her feet. While Rob shopped in the supermarket she wandered off and found a McDonald's, where she consumed a Big Mac and met some kids who were staying at a nearby holiday park. From the sound of it they were having a much better time than she was likely to have. When she told them she was staying in a poky little house right out in the country they had looked really sorry for her.

On the drive back to Gull Cottage her spirits began to sink again. To make things worse Rob was angry with her for disappearing. "One minute you were there," he said, "and the next you'd vanished off the face of the earth! You might at least have told me where you were going."

"I didn't *know* where I was going," Kezzie said. "I've never been here before."

"That's the trouble! I was afraid you'd get lost and wouldn't be able to find your way back to the car park."

"I'm not that stupid. If I couldn't find it I'd have asked someone."

"Yes, well..." Rob's anger began to subside. "You should have realized I'd be worried. It was very thoughtless of you."

"Sorry," said Kezzie, although she wasn't really. That Big Mac had been delicious, the best food she'd had in days.

He turned off the main road into the narrow lane that led to the creek. "We'd better call at the farm on our way back and tell Mrs Dent about the chimney smoking."

"And about the television," said Kezzie.

"Oh, yes." Rob chuckled, back to his usual

good humour. "Much more important as far as you kids are concerned."

The drive leading up to the farm was muddy and deeply rutted. Kezzie didn't particularly want to get out of the car, but she was afraid Rob might forget to mention the television if she wasn't there to remind him. She opened the door and lowered her pale blue trainers gingerly to the ground. They were practically new, a present from Rob and Jan on her birthday, and the most expensive footwear she had ever owned. She picked her way carefully across the cobbled yard, trying to avoid the puddles. As they neared the entrance a dog started to bark, making her jump.

Rob rang the bell and the barking increased to a frenzy. Kezzie moved behind him on the doorstep, fearing they might be attacked, but when Mrs Dent opened the door she saw that it was only the old black labrador they had met yesterday.

"Jasper, stay!" Mrs Dent caught hold of his collar. She looked apprehensively at Rob. "Is something wrong?"

"Nothing major," he said. "Just a couple of things that don't seem to be working properly."

"You'd better come in."

She looked nervous, Kezzie thought. What was she afraid they were going to complain about?

Mrs Dent led them into a big farmhouse kitchen with a stone-flagged floor and a long wooden table. "Sit down," she said. "Would you like a cup of tea?"

Rob said "yes" at once – he never said "no" to a cup of tea – but Kezzie shook her head. She was still too full of Big Mac. When Jasper came up to her, wagging his tail, she pretended not to notice. Dogs might be Baz's favourite animals but they certainly weren't hers!

"Now," said Mrs Dent, when she had poured out a rather stewed-looking brew from a teapot on the kitchen range, "what exactly is the problem?"

When Rob told her about the chimney and the television she seemed relieved, as if she had been expecting something much worse.

"Ah yes, the chimney does smoke a bit," she said calmly. "It always has done. I should have warned you. It's funny about the television, though. It's true I got it second-hand, but it was working perfectly when we put it in. I'd better get my nephew to look at it. He's good with all things electrical."

"Could it be soon, please?" said Rob. "You know what kids are like if they can't watch their favourite programmes."

"Wait, I'll give him a call." She disappeared into the yard outside. In the distance they heard her calling, "Gary! Gary, where are you?"

Rob said in a low voice, "It all seems very casual. Obviously she doesn't think a smoking chimney is anything to complain about."

Kezzie shrugged. "I don't think she's used to this letting game. Sounds like we're the first people who've ever stayed at the cottage."

"You could be right there."

Mrs Dent came back into the kitchen, followed by a tall young man wearing a crew-necked khaki sweater and frayed jeans. Not bad-looking, Kezzie thought, but a bit on the shy side, judging by the way he stood just inside the door, blushing and twisting his cap round and round in his hands.

"Gary will go back with you straight away," said Mrs Dent. "He'll sort out the TV, no problem."

Gary said hardly a word on the short drive down the road to Gull Cottage, and when Rob introduced him to Jan he whipped off his cap and blushed again. "Kezzie, show him where the television is," said Jan.

"Stupid," muttered Kezzie as she led him into the sitting room.

Gary gave her a surprised look, as if he thought he must have misheard her.

"I mean stupid showing you where the television is," she explained. "You must know this cottage a lot better than I do."

He shook his head. "Never been inside before."

"What?" Kezzie was amazed. "But it belongs to your aunt!"

"Always kept locked up. We used to dare

each other to break in here when we were kids, but…" He suddenly blushed twice as red as before, and avoided her eyes. "We usually chickened out."

"Why were you scared?" asked Kezzie. "What's wrong with the place?"

He looked ruffled. "It wasn't the place we were scared of, it was getting caught."

"By your aunt? She doesn't seem all that frightening."

"My uncle was still alive in those days and he had a very nasty temper. Used to whack us if we did anything we shouldn't." He glared at Kezzie. "Why are you so nosey?"

She shrugged. "I just think that if there's something wrong with the place you should've told us."

"Well, there isn't." He dropped to his knees in front of the television set and switched it on. "What's the trouble?"

"Lousy picture," said Kezzie. "Keeps breaking up and going into zig-zag lines, you know the sort of thing. Oh, and the sound is crackly."

The smiling face of a woman presenter appeared on the screen. A perfect picture, no lines, no crackles. Kezzie stared at it disbelievingly.

Rob came into the room, followed by Jan with the Squaller propped over her shoulder. "That was quick!" Rob said when he saw the screen. "Well done, Gary. What was the problem?"

"Wasn't one," mumbled Gary.

"Well, there was certainly one last night," said Jan, patting the Squaller's back. He had just been fed and for once he was quiet, dribbling contentedly against her collar. "It was a terrible picture."

"Must have been a temporary blip," said Rob. "Something in the atmosphere. Sorry to have troubled you unnecessarily."

"No trouble." Gary got to his feet and headed towards the hallway.

"At least let me make you a coffee now you're here," said Jan.

But Gary only shook his head and hurried out through the front door as if he couldn't wait to get away.

"Funny chap," commented Rob.

Kezzie moved quickly in pursuit of the vanishing Gary. "Hang on a minute," she called after him. "There's something I want to ask…"

She caught him up on the bridge. He scowled at her, obviously resentful at being delayed.

"Is this place haunted?" she asked abruptly.

"'Course not," he snapped. "Don't be stupid."

"Well, there's something wrong with it, I don't care what you say. It's got a funny atmosphere and – " she glanced down at the water – "and I don't like this bridge."

Gary turned pale. "Why d'you say that?"

"Because I don't. And neither does your aunt's dog." As she spoke she realized Gary had been edging away from her all the time they were speaking and by now had almost reached the road. "Nor do you, by the look of it. So what's going on?"

Gary didn't answer. He was already walking

fast up the road in the direction of the farm, hunching his shoulders as if he didn't want to hear any more.

Kezzie, watching him, shivered. "And another thing," she muttered under her breath. "It's always cold on this bridge. I bet it's cold even on a hot day. So you can't tell *me* it's not haunted, Gary Dent!"

Chapter 5
Dark Secrets

After lunch James said, "Dad, when we went down to the harbour we found a place where they hire out boats."

"Oh, yes?" Dad said warily. "What kind of boats?"

"All kinds. I got talking to a guy who works there and he said he'd hire us one as long as you were with us."

"James, you have to know what you're doing when you take out a boat. I don't know any more about sailing than you do. A couple of novices setting out to sea would be asking for trouble."

"I wasn't thinking of setting out to sea,"

said James. "But if we had a rowing boat we could explore the creek much better than we can on foot. And I can row, I'm sure I can. Anyone can *row*."

"We'll see," said Dad.

James was tempted to tell him what Dave Sadler had said about the cottage being haunted, but he was aware that Baz and Alison were listening and decided not to risk it. Instead he said, "I think I'll walk up to the village shop and see if they've got any books about Jacob's Creek. Local history, that sort of stuff. Anyone want to come?"

The others shook their heads. Kezzie muttered something rude about him and his boring old history books, but he pretended he hadn't heard. She had been in a foul mood ever since this morning, when she had given Dad the slip during their visit to Newport. James had overheard him telling Mum about it. "So much for your brilliant idea that she should help me with the shopping," Dad said; but Mum had only murmured no harm done and best to forget about it.

The village shop was part general store, part post office. They had a surprisingly good selection of local guide books, but to be honest he wasn't quite sure what he was looking for. It wasn't until he saw the title *The Secret History of the Isle of Wight* that he began to feel he was on the right track. The first page he opened said, "*The Island has a mysterious past, full of dark secrets...*" Just what he wanted! Luckily it was a paperback and not too expensive. He bought it and put it inside his anorak pocket.

As soon as he got back to Gull Cottage he went up to the room he shared with Baz and started to read. Most of the Island's secrets, according to the book, were connected with smuggling. Landing the contraband goods was a dangerous enough operation, but even more dangerous was transporting them across country without being caught by the Revenue Men. Intrigued, James read on, until he became aware of a disturbance downstairs. Raised voices, Alison complaining, Kezzie sounding furious, Dad trying to reason with them, the Squaller in full cry. With a sigh he put the book under his pillow and went down to investigate.

"The telly's not working again," Alison told him as soon as he appeared.

"Well, it was working all right this morning," said Mum, jiggling the Squaller up and down in an attempt to calm him. "Kezzie, you were here when Mrs Dent's nephew switched it on. You saw for yourself, there was nothing wrong with the picture then."

"It's this house," Kezzie muttered, glowering. "It makes things go wrong."

"Oh, don't be silly! What else has gone wrong?"

"Everything. I don't like it here. I want to go home."

"Now listen, all of you," said Dad in a tone of quiet desperation. "I'm sure there's a simple explanation. Perhaps there's a machine working somewhere that upsets the signals."

"What kind of machine?" Kezzie demanded. "There isn't another building for miles."

"There's the farm. Farms are very high

tech these days. They probably use machines for all sorts of jobs. Why don't some of you go and ask Mrs Dent?"

"Not me," Kezzie said quickly. "I'm not going near that place again. It took me hours this morning to clean the mud off my trainers."

James said, "I'll go, if you like."

"I'll come with you," Baz said unexpectedly.

As soon as they reached the farm James realized why Baz had been so keen to accompany him. It was because he wanted to see Mrs Dent's dog again. While Baz crouched by the kitchen range, stroking Jasper, James told her Dad's theory about the television and asked if there was any kind of machinery working at the moment that could be causing interference.

"None that I can think of," she said, avoiding his eyes. "Gary, you'd better have another look at it."

Her nephew threw down the newspaper he

was reading. "Can't tonight," he said shortly, getting to his feet. "Got to go out."

"You never said." His aunt looked disbelieving. "Where are you going?"

"Down the pub. Promised to meet Dave Sadler for a game of darts." He left the kitchen before she had time to protest.

She gave an embarrassed shrug. "Tell your father I'm sorry," she said to James. "I'll see what we can do about it tomorrow."

"Is that Dave Sadler from the boatyard?" James asked.

"What? Oh, yes. He and Gary went to school together. You've met Dave, have you?" She seemed glad to change the subject.

James nodded. "We're going to hire a rowing boat from him and explore the creek."

"That'll be nice." She glanced at Baz. "Your young brother's good with animals. You must bring him to see the horses some time."

Baz looked up at once. "You've got horses?"

"Two," she said. "They belong to my daughter, who's away at university. Can you ride?"

He stared at her as if he hadn't understood the question. James answered for him. "No, he can't. None of us can, I'm afraid. We live in a town, you see. We don't get much opportunity for riding."

"Pity," said Mrs Dent. "The horses could do with some exercise. Never mind, come up and see them anyway." She opened the door for them to go.

As they moved towards it Baz blurted out, "Tomorrow?"

"If you like. Better come in the morning, about eleven."

A delighted grin spread over Baz's face. "You see?" James said to him as they walked back up the lane. "This holiday isn't going to be as bad as you expected."

As they entered Gull Cottage Mum said, "Well done! What was it?"

"What was what?" asked James.

"The machine causing the interference. You must have found out what it was because the picture's perfect again now."

He opened the door of the sitting room and

looked inside. Sure enough, the others were slumped happily on the sofa, their eyes glued to the TV screen, Alison tucking into a bag of salt 'n' vinegar crisps. Harmony had been restored, no one was complaining, even the Squaller slept peacefully in his carry-cot. James closed the door on the tranquil scene.

"Well, it wasn't anything to do with us," he told his mother. "It must have got right by itself."

But later that night, when he lay in bed, he kept thinking of what Kezzie had said about the house making things go wrong. Gull Cottage seemed a strangely restless place even when nobody was moving about in it, full of small, unidentifiable noises.

Just when he was on the point of falling asleep he heard the sound of hoofbeats and was startled back into wakefulness. It sounded as if a horse – several horses – were coming down the lane at full tilt. That was the final straw, people riding around the countryside at dead of night! Had they no consideration for others? In desperation he pulled the bedclothes over his head.

Chapter 6
Hoofbeats in the Night

Kezzie lay rigid in bed, listening to the thunder of horses' hooves. More than one horse, by the sound of it, and galloping fast. But who would be stupid enough to go riding in the dark? It must be dangerous when you can't see where you're going, especially with so much water around.

Unless they had no riders. Perhaps they were runaways...

The hoofbeats stopped abruptly, as if the horses had drawn to a halt right outside Gull Cottage. Kezzie held her breath, but could hear only Alison snoring in the bunk above her. When she could bear the suspense no longer she slipped from her bed and padded over to the window. Her heart thudding in her chest, she lifted the curtain and peered out.

There was nothing there.

She could see clearly enough, by the light of a three-quarter moon, but the bridge was silent and deserted, not a horse in sight. On the opposite bank stood a strangely shaped tree, with gnarled branches and a hollowed-out trunk as if at some time it had been struck by lightning. In the moonlight it cast long shadows over the empty road. Shivering, she returned to bed and pulled the bedclothes up to her chin.

Had nobody heard the hoofbeats except herself? Something seemed to be keeping the Squaller awake. She could hear him whimpering in the distance, yet strangely no one seemed to be taking any notice. Usually Jan got up straight away but tonight she must be turning a deaf ear. Or perhaps she was sleeping heavily as well.

"I *hate* this place!" Kezzie muttered into

her pillow. And this was only the second night of the holiday.

Next morning she was first down to breakfast. Jan looked at her in astonishment. "Kezzie! This must be a record. Are you feeling all right?"

"Didn't sleep too good." Kezzie stopped by the Squaller's carry-cot and peered down at him. "Nor did he, I reckon. Must have kept you awake for hours."

"As a matter of fact he slept like a log. Best night we've had for weeks. Not a peep out of him."

"But I – " Kezzie stopped; then realized that Jan was looking enquiringly at her. "I thought I heard something. Must have been the wind."

But she was certain it hadn't been the wind. Had she imagined that ghostly crying in the night? And what about the hoofbeats? She longed to ask Jan if she too had heard the galloping horses but was afraid to in case the answer was no, which could only mean that she must be going round the bend. It was a bad sign when you started hearing things that weren't there.

She stared down at the Squaller, who lay on his back, gurgling contentedly and kicking his heels in the air. He was really rather an appealing baby when he wasn't crying. But it would be a mistake to let herself get too fond of him, or of Baz or Allie or any of the Tolliver family. In Kezzie's experience, as soon as you got fond of somebody they went away. She had made up her mind years ago she would never allow herself to get fond of anyone ever again.

When the others came down to breakfast James asked his father if they could go to the boatyard and hire a rowing boat. "Don't see why not," said Rob. "Who else wants to come?"

"Me," said Alison. "And Baz does too — don't you, Baz?"

Baz went scarlet. He seemed unable to speak and looked as if he might burst into tears.

Jan asked, "What's the matter, Baz? Are you afraid of the water?"

He shook his head. "'Tisn't that."

"What then?"

"Mrs Dent said – " He stopped, staring down at his plate.

"Oh, I know what's worrying him," said James. "Yesterday Mrs Dent said he could go and see the horses."

"Horses?" Kezzie said quickly. "What horses?"

"There are two on the farm. They belong to Mrs Dent's daughter." James said kindly to Baz, "Don't worry, I'll take you up there this afternoon. It doesn't have to be this morning."

"She said to come about eleven. She'll be expecting us." Baz looked more worried than ever.

"I'll take him," said Kezzie.

The others turned to stare at her, clearly surprised that she should offer to go to the farm this morning when yesterday she had flatly refused. But she had a good reason for changing her mind. If she could only find some rational explanation for those hoofbeats in the night it would prove she wasn't going round the bend.

She raised her chin defiantly. "One of us ought to tell Mrs Dent that the telly's working again, otherwise she might send someone to fix it," she pointed out.

"That's true," said Rob. "Good thinking, Kez."

Alison laughed. "I know why she wants to go to the farm! It's because she fancies Mrs Dent's nephew. She hopes that if she goes up there this morning she'll see him again."

Kezzie scowled furiously at her. "Don't be stupid! Come on, Baz." She pushed back her chair. "Let's go."

"It's too early," he protested. "She said eleven."

"We'll walk slowly."

They found Mrs Dent in the farmyard, carrying a basket of enormous eggs. "They're goose eggs," she said when Kezzie remarked on their size. "Would you like to take some back with you?"

Kezzie shook her head vigorously. She

didn't care for the idea of eggs laid by geese. Besides, they had very mucky-looking shells. She hated to think what they would taste like.

"Oh well, I'll just take these indoors and then we'll go up to the field."

While Mrs Dent unloaded the eggs Kezzie told her the TV was working again. "Looks like your father was right about the interference," she said. "I knew it couldn't be the set."

"How about *your* TV set?" Kezzie asked. "Do you get interference?"

Mrs Dent looked taken aback. "Sometimes," she said evasively.

But that wasn't the truth, Kezzie felt sure. So if it was caused by a machine working nearby why wasn't reception at the farm affected as well as at Gull Cottage? And why should Mrs Dent lie about it, anyway?

"Come, Jasper!" Mrs Dent called; and to Baz's obvious delight the large black labrador came lumbering after them.

As Kezzie had feared, the track leading to

the field where the horses were kept was rough and muddy. Mrs Dent noticed her concern. "If you plan to do much walking around here you need a good pair of wellingtons," she said.

Wellingtons! Kezzie wouldn't be seen dead in anything so naff. "I don't plan to walk anywhere if I can help it," she muttered.

As soon as the horses saw Mrs Dent they came up to the gate, tossing their heads. "The little grey mare was my daughter's first pony," she said. "She's more or less retired now, but the chestnut's still young and full of beans. Here, I've brought some carrots you can give them."

She showed Baz how to hold his hand out flat so that the horses could take the carrots easily. Kezzie was surprised how little fear he showed, considering he was so timid with humans. Personally she found the horses unnerving, with their large yellow teeth and flaring nostrils.

"Can they get out of the field by themselves?" she asked Mrs Dent.

"Only if someone's stupid enough to leave the gate open."

"What about your nephew? Does he ever ride them late at night?"

"Good heavens, no! He'd rather ride his motor-bike." Mrs Dent gave her a curious look. "Why do you ask?"

Kezzie shrugged. "No reason."

Luckily Mrs Dent seemed happy to drop the subject. She smiled at Baz. "You're a natural with animals. You should be a vet when you grow up."

From the look on Baz's face you'd have thought he'd won the lottery. With surprising boldness he said, "Mrs Dent, can I take your dog for a walk?"

"If you like. I warn you, though, Jasper's getting old. He won't want to go too far. If you come back with me to the house I'll give you his lead."

Kezzie groaned inwardly. Now they were landed with taking the wretched dog for a walk! And it had all been a wasted exercise anyway. If what Mrs Dent said was true these couldn't possibly have been the same horses she'd heard last night.

Unless someone had taken them secretly and returned them to the field before anyone noticed they were missing. But why should they do that? She had so much wanted to find some explanation for those hoofbeats. Because if she couldn't…

The alternative was too spooky even to bear thinking about.

Chapter 7
Up the Creek

James pulled on the oars, propelling the boat slowly but steadily up the calm waters of the creek. At the boatyard Dad had said, "Right, James. You said anyone can row so now's your chance to prove it." And as they left the slipway he and Alison had sat facing him, laughing their heads off while the boat went round in circles and James got madder and madder. But now, after nearly twenty minutes, he was definitely getting the hang of it. The only trouble was that his hands hurt and he was beginning to tire.

"Someone else like a go?" he offered.

Dad leaned back and tipped his hat over his

eyes. "No, it's OK. You can carry on," he said generously, while Alison, gazing over the side into the murky grey water, pretended she hadn't heard.

After a while James stopped and rested on his oars. It was very quiet in this part of the creek. All he could hear, now that he had stopped rowing, was the faint gurgle of water in the reeds and the cry of a swan flying overhead.

It was like old times, he thought, just Dad and Allie and himself. This was how it used to be before they started fostering. If only Mum were with them it would be perfect, but of course she couldn't come because of the Squaller. He felt rather guilty that he hadn't taken Baz to see the horses, as he'd promised. Still, Kezzie had offered to go with him, which was rather surprising...

There was a jolt as the boat drifted into the bank. Alison looked round, startled, and Dad raised his hat. "What happened?"

"Sorry," said James. "My mind wandered." He pushed hard with one oar until the boat was free. As they drifted back into mid-stream Dad sat up and looked around.

"Any idea where we are?" he asked.

"Not really. It doesn't look anything like the map."

"Do you mean we're lost?" Alison looked delighted.

"There should be an island round here somewhere," said James. "Perhaps I took a wrong turning."

"We seem to be coming to a dead end," said Dad. "I can see a jetty ahead of us, with a boat tied up, but no way through."

James glanced over his shoulder. It was a dead end all right, with nothing in sight except a muddy foreshore and a mass of over-hanging trees. At the end of the jetty a lone bird sat on a post, regarding them with a wary eye. As they drew nearer it flexed its long neck and clumsily took to the air.

"Suffering cats! Can't a man work in peace around here?"

A gruff voice rang out in the still air, surprising James so much that he lost his grip on one of the oars. As he reached out to grab it the boat tipped sideways and swung round at right angles to the bank, giving him a better view of the jetty. The vessel tied to it was a shabby cabin cruiser which looked as if it hadn't been to sea for years, and on its deck stood a large bearded man, glaring down at them. In his shapeless blue jersey and woollen hat he looked every bit as shabby and barnacle encrusted as his boat.

"We're sorry if we disturbed you," Dad said in his most conciliatory voice. "But I'm afraid we – er, seem to have lost our way."

"It's not me you disturbed. You realize that cormorant hadn't moved for a good fifteen minutes? If you hadn't come blundering along I could have finished him off."

Alison looked horrified. "Then I'm glad we did! You've no right to go round finishing off birds. That's cruel."

The man stared at her. "Finished off *drawing* him, I mean." He waved a pencil in the air.

"Oh, you're an artist!" said Alison, relieved.

"I thought you meant you were going to kill him."

"Killing birds is not my idea of fun. I spend most of my life trying to save them from ignorant folk who mess up the creek with their oil and their rubbish." He frowned down at them. "Where are you trying to get to, anyway?"

"Back to the boatyard, I think," said Dad. "We've only hired this boat for a couple of hours. James, you'd better let me take over."

James, who had been trying to turn the boat back in the right direction, was only too happy to change places with his father. As they struggled to keep their balance during this manoeuvre the bearded man watched them with a mixture of wonder and irritation. When they finally pulled away from the jetty James distinctly heard him mutter under his breath a curse on all blundering grockles.

"What a rude old man," said Alison as soon as they were out of earshot. "Anyway, he didn't look a bit like an artist, more like a tramp. Dad, do you think he lives on that boat?"

Dad didn't answer. He was too busy trying to look as if he were an experienced oarsman, when in fact he didn't seem to be any better at rowing than James. However James thought it best to say nothing in case he got landed with the job again. Now that he was facing in the opposite direction he could see clearly where he had taken the wrong course. "There's the island!" he exclaimed. "I must have gone left instead of right. Never mind, we'll know better next time."

"What do you mean, next time?" growled Dad, who was beginning to perspire. "You're not getting me in a boat again this holiday, that's for sure."

"Oh, but Dad—"

"No arguing. It's too much like hard work for my liking."

When they arrived back at the boatyard Dave Sadler asked, "How'd you get on?"

"Fine, fine," said Dad, hiding his reddened hands behind his back.

"We lost our way," said Alison, "and met an old man who lived on a boat. He said he was an artist."

"Oh, that'd be Solo O'Rourke," said Dave. "He paints wildlife pictures and sells them in the summer to the visitors."

"Why is he called Solo?" asked James.

"Because he lives alone and prefers his own company to anyone else's." Dave smiled. "Quite a character, old Solo. There's not much he don't know about the creek. If you can ever get him talking he's got a good few tales to tell about olden times."

"About the smugglers?" asked James.

"More than likely. There's some who say he's done a bit of smuggling himself in the past, but he don't travel far these days. That old boat of his is more or less rotting where it lies. Shall we be seeing you again this week?"

"Maybe," Dad said evasively. "Depends how busy we are."

If only he could take the boat out alone, James thought as they left the boatyard, he could visit Solo O'Rourke again. Then he might find out more about the smugglers, perhaps even about the history of Gull Cottage. The only alternative was to go on foot. With the aid of the map it shouldn't be too difficult to find his way overland.

There was no chance that afternoon, however, because Dad insisted on taking them to the waxwork museum at Brading, which was full of spooky happenings such as corpses rising out of coffins and people being murdered in their beds. In the clear light of day the idea of ghosts seemed more comical than frightening and they all had a good laugh.

But it was a different matter in Gull Cottage at midnight, when he woke with a start and sat up in bed, his heart pounding.

No, he hadn't imagined it. He could definitely hear hoofbeats, as he had last night, and they seemed to be coming closer and closer, until finally they stopped outside with a stamping of feet and a jangle of harness. He held his breath.

Was that a knock at the front door?

Not a very loud one. He decided he must be mistaken; but then it came again, a quiet insistent rapping as if someone wanted to attract attention without making too much noise about it. James waited, still holding his breath. Surely Mum or Dad must have heard. Why didn't they go to see who it was?

The rapping sounded again, even more demanding.

He flung back the quilt and went over to the door. Cautiously he opened it and looked out, hoping to find his parents already on their way downstairs. But in the pale light of the moon shining through the high window he saw that the landing was empty. No one else seemed to be stirring. James shivered. He pulled on his dressing-gown, but before he could creep along the landing to his parents' room the door next to his opened and Kezzie's face appeared, stark white in the moonlight.

"What's the matter?" she demanded.

"Nothing," said James. "I was just, er, going to the bathroom."

"I thought you were burglars." Her voice sounded shaky.

"Don't be daft, you wouldn't get burglars in a place like this." Then, as an afterthought, he asked, "Why, did you hear something?"

"Only you thumping about." She gave him a challenging look. "Go on then, if you're going."

James hesitated. To be honest, the last thing he wanted to do at this moment was venture downstairs. He said with a shrug, "It's OK. I don't think I'll bother."

"Now who's scared of burglars?"

"Not me! I've changed my mind, that's all."

"Go back to bed, then – and let the rest of us get some sleep." She went back into the room and closed the door.

James waited a few seconds, but he heard nothing more. No knocking, no movement of any kind. Perhaps the horsemen had heard them talking and gone away? He couldn't help thinking that Kezzie must have heard something too or she wouldn't have come to find out what it was – and it couldn't possibly have been him thumping about as she'd said because he hadn't made a sound. Uneasily he took off his dressing-gown and crept back into bed.

Oh, no! Something must have woken the Squaller. James lay awake for some while, listening to the noise of distant sobs and wondering why nobody seemed to be doing anything about it. The odd thing was that it didn't *sound* like the Squaller. It was such a strange, eerie sort of crying, not the hearty bellow of a baby demanding attention but more the frightened whimper of a baby in distress. He'd never heard the Squaller cry like that before, not even when he first came to live with them.

But that was stupid. One baby's cry sounds much like another's. Of course it was the Squaller, it *had* to be. There wasn't another baby in the house. James pulled the quilt up over his ears.

Chapter 8
The Woman on the Bridge

It was on the following afternoon that Kezzie saw the woman standing on the bridge.

It had been a difficult day right from the start, when she got up late and stumbled downstairs to find that everyone else had already finished breakfast and made their plans. "Nice of you to join us," Rob said when he saw her. "We thought you were going to stay in bed till lunchtime."

"Couldn't sleep," she grumbled. "Too much noise."

"I expect she means me," said James. "I had to get up in the night to go to the bathroom. Did I wake anyone else?"

They shook their heads.

You woke the Squaller, Kezzie wanted to say; but she was afraid Jan might say that the baby had slept like a log and didn't want to risk looking foolish again.

She helped herself to a piece of toast. Meeting James on the landing last night had been an awkward moment. She had almost told him about hearing the hoofbeats, but thank goodness she had stopped herself in time. James had no imagination. He would only say she was being fanciful. And if this morning she had admitted she couldn't sleep because she was afraid of ghosts – well, he would probably laugh and say it was because of their visit to the waxwork museum. No, best to keep quiet about it.

"So, Kezzie," said Jan. "What do *you* want to do today?"

She shrugged.

"The others are going ten-pin bowling this morning and after lunch we thought we'd all drive down to Blackgang Chine."

"To see the dinosaurs," Alison explained.

Kezzie pulled a face. "Dinosaurs are kids' stuff. I don't mind going bowling."

Jan looked relieved. "Right, then. That's settled."

But it wasn't really, because she'd got bored with the bowling and wandered off to play the fruit machines, which annoyed Rob. And then in the afternoon she flatly refused to go to Blackgang Chine, hoping they would leave her behind so that she could catch the bus into Newport and mooch round the shops. Unfortunately Jan said she didn't particularly want to go to Blackgang either, making the excuse that it wasn't easy toiling round an adventure park with the Squaller. And Baz got out of it by saying he would rather take Mrs Dent's dog for a walk. So Kezzie was stuck at Gull Cottage, whether she liked it or not.

To make matters worse, as soon as the others had gone Jan called her into the kitchen and said, "Sit down. I want to talk to you," which was a sure sign she intended to have what she called a "heart-to-heart".

Kezzie hated "heart-to-hearts", which in her opinion were just a way of trying to pry into your mind and find out your innermost secrets. She had no intention of telling anyone her innermost secrets, not even Jan. Anyway, by now they were so tightly locked away she could hardly remember what they were.

"I'd so hoped you would enjoy this holiday," Jan began. "I know this isn't exactly the sort of place you would choose to come to—"

"Hate it," growled Kezzie.

"Why? What don't you like about it?"

Dangerous moment. Kezzie would have loved to tell her *exactly* what she didn't like about it, but she knew Jan would only say she was being fanciful and there was no such thing as ghosts anyway. "Boring," she mumbled instead.

"Oh, Kezzie." Jan's voice was full of reproach. "But you are happy with us, aren't you?"

Kezzie was on her guard at once. Here

came the heart-to-heart, if she wasn't careful. She said quickly, "Yes, of course. It's just this place I can't stand. The sooner we go home the better as far as I'm concerned."

Jan was always pleased when she spoke of "home". Her face cleared. "Well, it'll only be for a few more days. And at least the rain's stopped. It's still a bit misty, but much too good to be sitting indoors, staring at the television."

Kezzie saw there would be no peace if she stayed around. Reluctantly she got to her feet. "I'll go after Baz," she said. "I'll help him take the dog for a walk."

Jan looked delighted. "What a good idea! If you hurry you'll catch him up at the farm."

She didn't hurry; but she still caught him up at the farm. He was hanging around the sheds where the calves were kept. "When I'm a vet," he told her, "I'm going to help calves get born."

Kezzie wrinkled her nose in disgust. "It's a messy business," she warned. "I've seen it on the telly."

"Gary says it's the best thing in the world."

She saw Mrs Dent's nephew forking hay off a truck on the other side of the yard. A pity he was so shy because he was really quite good-looking. "Our TV went funny again last night," she called out to him. "You'd better come and have another look at it."

He shook his head and went on working.

No doubt about it, he was determined not to come anywhere near the cottage if he could possibly help it. So much for her fatal charm, Kezzie thought dispiritedly. Actually the TV had righted itself after about half-an-hour, but during the time when it was on the blink she had felt uneasy. Even the Squaller seemed to have sensed something in the atmosphere.

"Come on," she said briskly to Baz. "If we're taking this dog for a walk let's get moving."

He went into the farmhouse and collected the lead from Mrs Dent. This was the third day he had taken Jasper for a walk and the labrador greeted him like an old friend. "You'd better tell me where you're going," Mrs Dent said when she came to the door to see them off.

"Oh, just round and about," Baz said vaguely. "Probably where we went yesterday."

"Well, take care. And don't make it too long a walk. Remember Jasper's not as young as he used to be." Mrs Dent went inside and shut the door.

"This place you went yesterday," Kezzie said as they walked down the drive from the farm. "I hope it wasn't too muddy?"

"Pretty muddy," Baz admitted.

"Then let's go somewhere else. How about up to the village?"

It was quite a long walk to the village; and when they got there Kezzie spent so much time in the general stores without buying anything that the woman behind the counter got ratty and they had to leave. On the way back Baz said that Jasper was fed up with being kept on the lead and persuaded her to take a path he was certain would take them back to the farm. As soon as they left the road he released Jasper, who plunged happily into the undergrowth.

The path took them a devious route through woods and over stiles, getting wetter and muddier by the minute. Kezzie stared down at her beautiful trainers, now barely recognizable. "They're ruined!" she exclaimed. "I'm not going another step."

But Baz insisted he knew where he was and if they carried on down the path they would come to the farm.

"You carry on if you want," said Kezzie. "I'm going back to the road."

She expected Baz to follow her, but he didn't. As she walked back along the way she had come her conscience gave her a few guilty stabs. After all, she was older than Baz and supposed to be looking after him. But that was Tolliver thinking again. Why *should* she feel responsible for Baz? He wasn't her real brother.

The trouble was she couldn't find the road. Instead she came to the river and decided to follow that instead, hoping that eventually it would bring her out somewhere near Gull Cottage. But it was becoming increasingly misty and she began to wonder if she was lost.

Then, to her relief, the scene began to look familiar. Surely that strangely-shaped oak with the hollow trunk was the same tree she could see from her bedroom window? But it was on the opposite bank, which meant she had somehow got herself on to the wrong side of the river, the same side as Gull Cottage. No wonder she hadn't been able to find the road!

She quickened her step as ahead of her she saw the bridge, wreathed in mist. Nearly there! Only a few more steps and she would reach Gull Cottage...

Kezzie stopped dead.

A woman stood on the bridge. A youngish woman with long dark hair, staring at the house. A woman who appeared to have no legs, just her head and body floating above the ground...

Kezzie felt paralysed, unable even to breathe. Then, slowly, the woman turned to look straight at her. Her eyes were dark and very sad. She raised a hand as if in greeting and started to glide across the bridge.

"No," murmured Kezzie under her breath. "Oh, no. Please *no*!" And she raised her arm as if trying to stop the apparition in its tracks.

But the ghostly figure kept on coming slowly, steadily, over the bridge towards her. Nothing, it seemed, could halt its silent progress.

"No!" Kezzie's shout rang out. "That bridge is dangerous!"

The woman appeared to hesitate. She looked uncertain, even fearful, and to her horror Kezzie realized she was standing exactly above the point where she had first seen the face in the water. Was the woman about to re-live the moment when she plunged to her death? Panicking, Kezzie knew only that she must stop her trying to come any further.

"Please go back," she begged. "*Go back or you'll be drowned!*"

The woman stared at her, her mouth an open O of astonishment.

Kezzie could bear it no longer. With a groan she turned and ran into Gull Cottage. She slammed the door shut and leaned against it, breathing heavily.

Jan came out of the kitchen. "Hello, did you have a nice walk?"

Kezzie stared at her, unable to speak.

"What on earth's the matter? You look as if you've seen a ghost."

"It was a woman…" Kezzie gulped. "She didn't have any legs."

"Poor soul," said Jan. "Still, there's no need to go upsetting yourself about it. Where's Baz?"

"Taking Mrs Dent's dog back." Her breathing began to return to normal. Useless trying to explain to Jan that the woman had not been in a wheelchair or on crutches, but *floating above the ground*. Jan would never believe her. Nobody would. Nobody in their right minds.

Oh, yes, it had been a very difficult day. From now on, Kezzie resolved, she would not set a foot outside the cottage if she could possibly help it. It wasn't safe.

The trouble was, she didn't feel particularly safe *inside* the cottage either.

Chapter 9
Solo O'Rourke

With the folded map under his arm James went into the sitting room and said, "I thought I might explore a bit further this morning."

"That's a good idea," said Dad. "You can take Baz with you. Baz, are you walking Mrs Dent's dog again today?"

Baz looked doubtful. "She said I could, as long as I didn't go too far. Yesterday – well, me and Kez got a bit lost and I was late taking him back. Mrs Dent wasn't too pleased."

"I expect she was worried," Mum said. "And I'd have been worried too, if I'd known. Kezzie, you never mentioned you got lost?"

Kezzie, slumped in a chair with a magazine, didn't look up. "Ruined my trainers," she muttered. "This place is one large bog. You won't catch me going for a walk round here again."

"Well, I certainly don't want Baz roaming around the countryside on his own, dog or no dog. He'll have to go with James or not at all."

"I'll go too," said Alison. "I like exploring."

James's heart sank. Last night he had heard the hoofbeats again, and he was now convinced they were not made by real, flesh-and-blood horses but by the shades of horses who had galloped this way a hundred years ago or more. And crossed the bridge to the cottage. And knocked at the door. But for what reason?

The answer had something to do with smuggling, he felt sure. That's why he had looked at the map to find where Solo O'Rourke lived, so that he could go and have a private chat with him, instead of which he was lumbered with two kids and a dog. Company was the last thing he'd wanted on this particular expedition, but it would be difficult to refuse without arousing suspicion.

"Oh, all right," he said resignedly. "Baz, you'd better go and fetch the dog first. There's no point in us all going up to the farm. I'll wait for you outside."

Soon Alison came to join him, trussed up in her anorak like a Christmas parcel. "I tried to make Kezzie come with us," she told James, "but she says she's not leaving the house today."

"Good," said James shortly. "Here comes Baz. Now we can get started."

He led them along the path beside the river, setting such a fast pace that the two younger ones had a hard job keeping up. Eventually Baz protested that Jasper was lagging behind.

"He likes to have a good sniff," he explained.

James sighed impatiently, but had to admit that the slower pace gave them more time to take in their surroundings. The path took them away from the river bank and into a copse where primroses grew wild, like a carpet spread out among the trees. At one point he spotted a squirrel scampering along a willow branch and pointed it out to the others.

"That wasn't a squirrel," said Alison. "Squirrels are grey. It must have been a baby fox."

"Foxes don't climb trees," Baz told her.

"It wasn't a squirrel," she insisted. "We've got squirrels in our garden at home and they don't look like that."

"Well, it wasn't a fox."

"Was!"

"Wasn't!"

This argument continued for some time, until James told them to belt up.

At last they came within sight of the jetty. Alison stopped dead. "Oh, look!" she exclaimed. "This is where we came the other day. There's the boat where that rude old man lives. How amazing!"

"Amazing," James echoed, secretly congratulating himself on finding it so easily. "I wonder if he's at home."

"I hope not," Alison said fervently. "I don't want to meet *him* again."

"Then you shouldn't have come here," said a gruff voice.

They swung round to see Solo O'Rourke, who seemed to specialize in surprise appearances, come from behind a tree. He stood before them on the path, arms folded and an unwelcoming glare in his fierce blue eyes.

"Er, good morning," said James.

Solo said nothing, but went on glaring at them. All James's hopes of having a useful conversation seemed doomed, until Jasper came crashing out of the undergrowth and went straight up to the old man, wagging his tail with pleasure.

"Well, if it isn't Mrs Dent's labrador!" He bent to pat the dog's head. "And what are you doing with these young gatecrashers, Jasper?"

Surprisingly, it was Baz who spoke up. "Mrs Dent lets me take him for walks. We're staying in her cottage."

"And we haven't crashed into any gates," Alison assured him earnestly. "We just walked along the path. We saw a fox climb up a tree."

"It was a squirrel," said Baz. "She thought it was a fox because it was a foxy colour."

"Oh, don't start that again!" pleaded James.

"Wait here," said Solo O'Rourke.

He climbed on to his boat and went into the cabin. A minute later he reappeared with a large pad and turned over the pages until he came to a watercolour sketch of a small furry creature with tufted ears. "Does that look anything like it?"

"Yes!" said Baz and Alison in unison.

"Then you saw a red squirrel. And you were lucky, because they're much shyer than grey ones and spend most of their time in the trees. The Island is one of the few places left in Britain where you can find red squirrels. If a grey one stows away on a ferry it gets shipped straight back to the mainland, because when the greys invade their territory the reds die out."

Baz stared at the painting. "That's brilliant. I wish I could paint like that."

"He's mad about animals," Alison told Solo O'Rourke. "When he grows up he wants to be a vet." She seemed to have lost her previous dislike of the old man.

James cleared his throat. "Dave Sadler at the boatyard told us you know a lot about this creek, Mr O'Rourke. He said you had some good stories to tell."

The old man took out a pipe and began filling it with tobacco from a tin. "I've got a few."

James glanced warily at Baz and Alison, but they were busy looking through the sketch-pad. "Was there much smuggling round here in olden times?"

"Aye, plenty! My ancestor was one of the original Jacob's gang who used to operate in these parts. Silent O'Rourke was his name, so called because he never grassed on his mates. Unlike one I could mention."

"Who?"

"Man by the name of Stew Baker." He struck a match and lit his pipe. "Story goes that one dark night the gang planned to move a haul of brandy from a hide near the creek to a safe house, but Stew Baker tipped off the

Preventive men."

"Who were the Preventive men? Do you mean Customs Officers?"

Solo nodded. "Set an ambush, they did, and caught nearly the whole gang. Some escaped, though. And the one that shopped them paid for it afterwards. Oh yes, they got their revenge all right."

"How?"

"Went visiting in the moonlight with an axe."

James swallowed hard. "When they went visiting – were they on horseback?"

The old man took the pipe out of his mouth and stared at him. "Where did you say you were staying?"

"At Gull Cottage. It belongs to Mrs Dent."

"Oh, aye." He pulled thoughtfully on his pipe.

"Well, were they? On horseback, I mean."

"Maybe. Maybe they were on foot. I dis-remember that bit." He glanced at Baz and Alison, who were admiring a painting of a seabird. "That's a red merganser," he said.

"It's a kind of duck. You want to get yourselves a good bird book. Then you'll know what you're looking at."

Useless trying to get any more information out of him. He had clammed up as soon as he realized where they were staying – and that told James all he needed to know. Gull Cottage was haunted all right, by the men on horseback who came seeking revenge on the man who once lived there. The man called Stew Baker.

Chapter 10
A Ghoulish Story

Kezzie was dead scared. At least, half of her was. The other, more sensible, half kept telling her not to be so stupid, there was no such thing as ghosts and it must have been the mist that made it look as if the woman had no legs. There was often that kind of a mist over the creek. She had seen it again this morning. It lay above over the water in wispy streaks, like a Chinese painting the Tollivers had at home of a mountain top showing above the clouds. If she hadn't run indoors in such a panic she would have seen that the mist over the bridge was level with the woman's legs, which was why it looked as if she hadn't any.

Yes, that was the only logical explanation.

She had almost convinced herself that the sensible side of her was right when the others came back from their walk.

"Guess what!" said Alison, bursting into the sitting room. "Jasper won't cross the bridge again."

"Perhaps he's afraid of water," suggested Jan, who was giving the Squaller his bottle.

"He loves water. He goes right in up to his neck if you throw a stick for him. But when we got to the bridge all his fur went up on his back and he just refused to cross. Baz is taking him back to the farm." She threw herself on to the sofa beside Kezzie. "What are you watching?"

"Some stupid cartoon," growled Kezzie, who had not taken her eyes off the TV screen since Alison came into the room. She dared not, in case she gave herself away. What Alison had said confirmed her worst suspicions. So the bridge *is* haunted, said her non-sensible half, back in control. Told you so!

"Where's James?" asked Jan, removing the bottle from the Squaller's mouth.

"Gone up to his room. He says he wants to read in peace."

At the word "peace" the Squaller opened his mouth into a square and began to bawl. Jan quickly propped him over her shoulder and started patting his back. "There, there," she said comfortingly. But he went on bawling just the same.

Then the TV went peculiar.

Kezzie sprang to her feet. That was the final straw! Legless women, dogs that wouldn't cross bridges – and now haunted TV screens. "I'm getting out of here," she muttered.

"Where are you going?" asked Jan, still trying to quieten the Squaller.

"Up to the farm with Baz."

"Good idea. You're looking much too pale."

Anyone would look pale, Kezzie thought, if they'd seen what she'd seen. But her real reason for wanting to go out was because she needed some answers – and there was only one person she could think of who might be able to supply them. Oh, not Mrs Dent. Mrs Dent was far too anxious to make out there was nothing wrong with her cottage. But Mrs Dent's nephew Gary…

As she reached the door Jan called after her, "Don't be too long. It's nearly lunchtime."

She put on her jacket and went outside. For a moment she hesitated, hating the idea of having to cross the bridge. Summoning all her courage she hurried over it as fast as she could and soon caught up with the dawdling Baz.

He looked at her in surprise. "I thought you had a headache?"

"Yeah, I do. That's why I need some fresh air. Anyway, you shouldn't go out alone."

"Why? I'm not scared."

"Then you should be," she muttered as she set off at a cracking pace up the road.

The shameful truth was that she needed Baz's company more than he needed hers. She was afraid to go out alone in case she saw the woman again. Next time she wanted to have someone with her so that she could be sure she wasn't going mad.

"Can't you slow down a bit?" Baz grumbled, following with Jasper. "You're as bad as James."

But she did not slow down until she reached the farm. As soon as she came within sight of the house she left Baz and went in search of Mrs Dent's nephew. She found him in the cowshed, eating a cheese sandwich. He started guiltily when he saw her and said, "I was just having my nammet."

"Nammet?"

"That's Isle of Wight for a snack," he explained. "I didn't have time to eat it earlier. Aunt Mary's kept me hard at it this morning."

"I bet she's a slavedriver." Kezzie smiled at him conspiratorially. If she could only get him on her side he was far more likely to tell her what she wanted to know. "Why don't you get another job?"

He shrugged. "No jobs to be had. Anyway, she's not too bad. I could do with a bit of help, but of course that's out of the question. Not enough money."

"I thought farmers were supposed to be rich?"

"Ha, that's a good one! Why else do you think she wanted to let the cottage?"

Kezzie leaned against the cowshed door, digging her hands into her pockets. "Do you get a lot of visitors staying in the cottage?" she asked casually.

"Nope." He struggled to snap the lid shut on the empty sandwich-box. "Matter of fact, you're the first."

"The first this year – or the first ever?"

"The first ever. She's never let it before."

"Why's that?" Kezzie asked innocently. "Because it's haunted?"

He looked annoyed. "I told you, that's rubbish."

"You can't fool me, Gary Dent." She paused for dramatic effect. "I've seen the ghost."

He stared at her in disbelief. "You can't have! Nobody's ever actually *seen* it, not ever."

"Well, I have. A woman, quite young, with long dark hair. I saw her yesterday, standing on the bridge."

Gary went whiter than any ghost and he seemed incapable of speech.

"I'm right, aren't I?" Kezzie said. "About it being a woman, I mean."

He gulped. "You could be."

"So who was she and why does she haunt Gull Cottage?"

"You don't want to hear that. It's a pretty ghoulish story."

"I don't care how ghoulish it is." She fixed him with a purposeful stare. "If I'm the only person in the world ever to have seen this ghost I think I have a right to know who she is. Don't you?"

Gary's face turned from white to red. He shuffled his feet and looked uncomfortable. "Well, the fact is she got murdered – oh, hundreds of years ago."

"By some men on horseback?"

"How'd you know that?" He looked astonished.

"Because I've heard them, late at night when I've been trying to sleep. They come thundering up the lane and then knock on the door." She could feel herself getting angry. Knowing she had been right about the woman on the bridge only made things worse. "Frankly, I don't think people should be allowed to let haunted cottages. There ought to be a law against it."

"You can't blame my aunt," said Gary. "OK, so everyone knows that the cottage is *supposed* to be haunted, but nobody's actually seen or heard anything for years. She thought it would be safe – and, like I said, she needs the money."

Kezzie regarded him thoughtfully. "What actually happened to this woman?"

He looked uncomfortable. "The story goes that when the men came to the house they took the baby—"

"What baby?"

"Her baby. She followed them to try and get it back and that's when they killed her."

Kezzie's brain went into overdrive. So there had been a baby ... a baby who cried in the night, but who wasn't the Squaller. That was one mystery explained.

"How did they kill her?" she asked.

"They pushed her into the river and held her under till she drowned."

Kezzie felt sick. So sick she had to hold on to the cowshed door for support. That face in the water, the face she had seen the day they arrived, with the open O for a mouth, just like somebody drowning...

"I warned you it was ghoulish," Gary said.

"What happened to the baby after its mother was killed?" she asked faintly.

Gary shrugged. "Did you really see a woman on the bridge?"

"Yeah, I did." She couldn't bring herself to say another word, but turned around and stumbled across the yard towards the house.

Baz was waiting for her. "I thought you'd gone without me," he said.

"I went to see Gary Dent." She marched on down the drive without stopping.

"Why?" He ran after her. "Is it is true, what Alison said? Do you fancy him?"

"No, I don't!" she said fiercely. "I never want to see him again."

Baz peered into her face. "You look awful. Is your headache worse?"

"Yeah. Much worse."

Tactfully he kept quiet for the rest of the way.

As soon as they got back to Gull Cottage she went to look at the Squaller sleeping in his carry-cot. "It's because of you this house is haunted," she told him. "The ghost knows you're here and it's upsetting her. She thinks you're *her* baby and that's why she's come back."

"Who's come back?" asked James, overhearing as he came into the room.

"Dracula's mother," snapped Kezzie.

James was the last person she could confide in. He would only say that Gary's story had been a load of old rubbish and if she believed that she'd believe anything. And what's more she might have agreed with him, if she hadn't seen with her own eyes the woman on the bridge.

Chapter 11
Spooks in the Night

When James came back from the village he found his parents in the kitchen. Both looked troubled. "I was just telling your father," Mum said in a low voice, "Kezzie's behaving most oddly. She says this place is dangerous and we ought not to spend another night here, but she won't tell me why. Now she's in the other room, sulking."

"Too bad," said Dad. "This is supposed to be a family holiday and if she wants to be part of our family then she must learn to accept things gracefully, even if they're not to her liking."

"I'm not sure that she does want to be part of our family any more," Mum said sadly.

"It's such a shame, because the holiday is doing wonders for Baz. He's been a different boy since we came here."

"Where is he now?" asked James.

"He went down to the quay with Allie to feed the ducks."

"I'll go and find them. I just bought a bird-spotting book in the village, so if I give it to Baz he can start using it straight away."

On his way to the harbour he passed a young woman wearing a shapeless ankle-length dress with a shawl around her shoulders. She looked cold and rather out-of-place, he thought, in this seafaring haven where everyone else wore jeans and sweaters and boots. But he hardly gave her a second glance as he went on his way.

He saw Dave Sadler working in the yard and called out, "Have you seen my brother and sister?"

"They're down by the slipway." Dave straightened and came over to him. "By the way, I've got a bone to pick with you."

"A bone?"

"Yeah. Gary Dent told me that sister of

yours has been hanging around the farm, asking questions."

"Who – Allie?" James was amazed.

"No, the older one." Dave leaned against the boatyard wall. "She told Gary she'd seen spooks on the bridge, which is a load of rubbish. I mean, there's always been stories about the place but nobody's ever actually *seen* anything." He gave James a hard look. "Have you been trying to scare her?"

James was indignant. "No, of course not."

"Dad was right, I shouldn't have told you it was haunted that first day you came. It was only a joke, you know. You shouldn't have taken me seriously."

"I didn't! I never said a word to anyone."

"Well, she must have got it from somewhere." Dave suddenly grinned. "You want to be careful. I used to tease my sister when she was younger and now she doesn't believe a word I say." He turned away from the wall. "Let us know if you and your dad want to go out rowing again."

James walked on, his mind buzzing with

what Dave had just told him. If Kezzie had seen spooks on the bridge why hadn't she said anything? Or had she been trying to tell Mum about it when she said this place was dangerous?

He found Baz and Allie standing up to the tops of their boots in mud, competing to find the deepest puddle. Baz was delighted with the bird book and soon identified the birds he'd been feeding as shelduck.

When they returned to Gull Cottage James went in search of Kezzie. He found her slumped on the sofa, gloomily watching a cartoon, and sat in the armchair opposite. "Why don't you want to go out?" he asked. "Are you scared of something?"

"Shut up, James."

"Mum said you thought this place was dangerous. Is it because—?"

"I said *shut up*!" she muttered through clenched teeth. "My head aches enough already without you banging on."

"I'm not surprised. It's unhealthy to stop indoors all the—"

"Must you be so flaming pompous?" She glared at him furiously. "You really are the biggest pain I've ever met, James Tolliver. Now shove off and let me watch the telly in peace."

Stung, he picked up the nearest book, which happened to be *The Secret History of the Isle of Wight*. Somehow with Kezzie he always ended up feeling a first-class prig. Still smarting, he opened the book and pretended to read.

Suddenly Kezzie groaned. "Oh, not again!"

James looked up. "What's the matter now?" he demanded.

She pointed wordlessly at the TV screen.

He glanced at it and saw the familiar jazzy image, like a badly-knitted pullover. "Must be that machine again," he said shortly.

"It's not a machine," said Kezzie. "It's the Squaller. Can't you hear him?"

The baby was in the kitchen with Mum, but his fretful cries were clearly audible even in the living room.

James frowned. "What do you mean, it's

the Squaller?"

"It happens whenever he cries. Haven't you noticed?"

"He only cries because he's upset by the TV going wrong."

"Well, it can't have upset him this time. He's not even in the same room." Kezzie shook her head. "No, the interference doesn't begin until *after* the Squaller starts crying, not the other way round. He's the 'something in the atmosphere' that makes it happen."

"That's impossible. He's not a machine."

"You just don't get it, do you?" Kezzie's thin lips shut like a trap.

James was dangerously near losing his temper. "It's typical of you to blame the Squaller," he snapped. "You've always resented him."

"What?" Kezzie's green eyes widened.

"Poor little mite, he can't help the way he is. If you'd been left on the steps of a church you'd probably cry a lot as well! You ought to have some sympathy for him, not be always criticizing him the way you do."

"I'm *not* criticizing him!" she retorted. "I'm just trying to tell you why the telly keeps going wrong—"

"Exactly! You're saying it's his fault."

"No! I'm not *blaming* him. It isn't something he can help. It just … happens."

"That's rubbish!" He sprang to his feet and stood staring down at her. "You just want to go back to London, that's all it is. You're bored and you can't stand the rest of us having a good time. Well, it won't work! We're staying until the end of the holiday, whether you like it or not."

He didn't give her a chance to answer back, but turned on his heel and walked out of the room. Not wanting to go into the kitchen, where the Squaller was still yelling his head off, he opened the front door and walked fast down the path. He didn't know where he was going, only that he needed to get away from Gull Cottage.

When he reached the bridge he paused and leaned over the low stone wall, staring into the water. Kezzie made him so mad. He'd tried to be sympathetic, tried to get her to tell him what was troubling her, and all she'd done was accuse him of being pompous. And as for that rubbish about the Squaller making the television go wrong…

James shivered; then realized where he was standing. *She told Gary she'd seen spooks on the bridge*… He straightened and was about to move away when his eye was caught by something lying beneath the water, a pale round shape like a reflection of the moon.

Or a face, staring up at him. The face of a woman…

For a moment he was transfixed, unable to breathe. But even as he watched the image broke into tiny ripples and was lost. Must have been an optical illusion, he told himself. Anyway, whatever it was, it had nothing to do with horse-riders in the night. They were the real spooks, not some vague shape swimming in the water.

Even so, he walked away from the bridge as quickly as he could.

Chapter 12
Keeping Watch

Kezzie sat by the bedroom window, a coat over her pyjamas, staring out over the moonlit creek. It was gone eleven, but she couldn't sleep. She wouldn't be able to sleep ever again as long as they stayed in Gull Cottage.

"Kezzie?" Alison raised her head to peer into the semi-darkness. "Why are you sitting over by the window?"

"Keeping watch," said Kezzie.

"What for?"

"Nothing in particular. Go back to sleep."

"I can't." Alison swung her legs over the side of the bunk and sat with them dangling.

"James says you're not enjoying this holiday. He says you find us boring and don't want to be part of our family any more."

Kezzie smiled grimly to herself in the dark. "James doesn't know what he's talking about."

"He does usually."

"Well, this time he's wrong. Take my word for it."

Alison said jerkily, "It won't be the same if you go. I like having you and Baz and the baby around. It's more fun, being part of a big family."

A big family. It sounded good, sort of cosy and fun, but what Alison didn't realize was that the bigger the family the more likely it was to get broken up. Kezzie knew that from experience. She'd already come from one big family; and now she was supposed to be part of another. But for how long?

"You don't *want* to leave, do you?" Alison pleaded.

Kezzie shrugged. "All the same to me."

Don't get too attached, that was her motto.

The Tollivers were OK, but they had their drawbacks – and dragging their kids away on holiday to haunted houses was one of them! She turned back to look out of the window – and immediately stiffened.

The ghost woman was back, standing on the river bank with her gaze fixed on Gull Cottage.

"What is it?" Alison demanded. "What have you seen?"

Kezzie didn't answer. She was too busy trying to make out if the woman had legs, or if she was still floating above the ground, but it was impossible to see clearly. The moonlight dappled everything with patches of light and dark, and where the ghost woman stood, close to the stricken oak, was half in shadow.

Alison slid off the bunk and came to stand beside her, a reassuringly solid little figure in her winceyette pyjamas. "Is someone there?" she whispered hoarsely.

"Yes, over by that tree."

Alison peered out. "I can't see anyone."

"It's a woman. Be careful, she's looking right at us."

But at that moment the moon disappeared behind a cloud and everything went dark.

"You're imagining things," said Alison. "There's no one there."

"I tell you there was! And I've seen her before, on the bridge. I think she's watching this house."

"Why?"

"I'm not sure. It may be something to do with the baby…"

"Oh, Kezzie! James is right, you are mad." Alison turned and climbed back into her bunk. "We're in the middle of nowhere here. It's not like the town. People just don't go wandering around the countryside at this time of night."

Kezzie was filled with despair. She had so much wanted Alison to see the ghost woman. Then she could have been sure it wasn't just her imagination. But Alison had seen nothing. So what did that prove?

"Come to bed," Alison pleaded. "You'll catch cold if you sit there much longer."

Kezzie cast one last look out of the window,

but although the moon had come out again she could see no one standing under the tree. With a sigh she slipped off her coat and got back into the bunk. She wished now she hadn't told Alison that bit about the baby. Voicing her fear only made it worse, for she was convinced that the Squaller was in danger. It was his presence in the house that had awoken the ghost, and now the ghost would not be at rest until…

Until what?

Uneasily she drew the quilt over her ears and closed her eyes.

Sleep was a long time coming, but at last it did, only to be shattered a short while later when she was awoken by muffled sounds outside the window. She sat bolt upright, her heart thudding in her chest. Had she missed the hoofbeats? She could hear a huffing and a puffing and a faint jingle of harness, as if several horses were breathing heavily and shaking their heads. Next came a distant knocking, followed by the click of a latch.

Kezzie slipped from her bunk and went to

listen at the door. Shivering, she heard the heavy tread of several men moving through the house...

They were coming upstairs!

Her heart seemed to have stopped beating altogether. She pressed her ear against the door, holding her breath. From outside on the landing came the creak of a floorboard, followed by a whispered oath, as if someone were coming closer and closer. Any minute now they would surely reach her room...

Then, suddenly, the movement stopped and she heard whispering, as if the intruders were consulting with each other. She knew exactly what they were doing. They were looking for the baby! A wave of anger swept over her, banishing her fear. Without stopping to think she flung open the door and stepped out on to the landing.

There was nothing there.

Nothing visible, that is. But there was definitely *something*. She could feel it all around her, like an evil, swirling fog. Not a person but a presence – a menacing, dangerous presence, filling the landing with its foul breath and whispered threats.

"Go away!" she commanded in a low voice. "We don't want you here."

But the whispering only got louder and louder, until it seemed to fill her head. She pressed her hands over her ears to shut it out, while the invisible fog went on rolling like a tide towards the room where Jan and Rob were sleeping with the baby beside them in the cot.

"No! He's not your baby, he's ours..."

Kezzie began to move, but her legs seemed paralysed and she needed all her strength to put one in front of the other, as if she were wading through quicksand. Eventually she managed to reach the door and put her back against it, spreading out her arms to bar the way.

"You've got the wrong one, I tell you. Leave him alone!"

The fog rose up, almost suffocating her. She put a hand over her mouth and pressed back against the door, but it went on billowing around her and the whispering increased until it became a babble. She shrank back, no longer barring the way but using both arms to protect herself, until suddenly, without warning, the door burst open and she fell backwards into the room.

"What the – !" Rob's voice came out of the dark. He switched on the light. "Kezzie?"

Kezzie, sprawled on the floor, curled herself up in a ball for protection. "Watch out, they're coming in here!"

"Who?" asked Rob. "What on earth are you talking about?"

"I tried to stop them but they're too strong for me. Oh, don't let them take the baby! *Please* don't let them take the baby!"

Chapter 13
Just a Bad Dream

When the crash came James lowered the quilt. He had covered his ears when he first heard the hoofbeats, but the crash was too loud to be ignored; and it was followed by the sound of raised voices. Curious, he sat up.

"James?" Baz asked sleepily from the other side of the room. "Did you fall out of bed?"

The crash must have been loud to wake even Baz. "No, it wasn't me," said James. "I think it came from the landing."

He switched on the lamp, got out of bed and padded over to the door. When he opened it and looked outside he saw light streaming out from Mum and Dad's room. The voices he heard must have been theirs, now joined by the Squaller's fretful whimpering.

Alison appeared beside him. "What's going on?" she asked, rubbing her eyes.

"I don't know. We'd better find out."

He entered his parents' room with Alison and Baz close on his heels, but they all three stopped short when they saw Kezzie curled up on the floor with her arms over her head. Mum knelt beside her, murmuring words of comfort.

"What happened?" asked James.

"Kezzie fell into the room." Dad was standing by the cot, trying to quieten the Squaller. "Gave us a bit of a fright."

"Was she sleepwalking?" Alison asked.

"No, she just had a bad dream," said Mum. And when Kezzie muttered a protest she said, "Ssssh, it's all right. There's nobody there, I promise you."

"But the baby…" moaned Kezzie.

"The baby's quite safe. Can't you hear him?"

"She was worried about Brandon earlier,"

said Alison. "She said there was a woman outside watching the house…"

"Quiet, Allie," Mum said quickly, frowning at her.

"Go back to bed, all of you," said Dad. "No need to make a fuss."

"Is Kezzie coming back to bed?" asked Alison.

"Later. Now go," said Mum, in a tone that left no room for argument.

Reluctantly Alison left the room, followed by Baz and finally James. He lay awake for a long time, thinking about Kezzie crouched in a quivering heap on the floor. It was unlike her to go to pieces like that. Normally nothing seemed to scare her. What could possibly have reduced her to such a state of abject terror?

Next morning, when he found Mum alone in the kitchen, he asked if Kezzie really had had a nightmare. "She says not," Mum told him with a sigh. "But in the circumstances I'm pretty sure it must have been."

"How do you mean, in the circumstances?"

"Well … we don't know a great deal about Kezzie's life before she was taken into care, but we do know that she was the oldest of five children. According to the reports she looked after the younger ones more or less single-handed after her father died and was particularly attached to her baby brother. It must have broken her heart when the family was split up."

"I always thought she didn't like babies?"

Mum shook her head. "Just a defence mechanism. She's lost too much to risk going through it all again. That's why she won't let herself become too attached to Brandon – or at least, she's tried not to. But what happened last night made me realize how deep these things go. Apparently the nightmare was all about somebody coming into the house with the intention of taking the baby, which must date back to when she went through a similar experience. That's why I say it's not surprising in the circumstances."

James felt guilty and ashamed. If he'd known before about Kezzie's past history he'd never have said what he did about her hating the Squaller. He resolved that in future he'd make a real effort to be nicer to her, but when she finally came downstairs that morning she was in a dark and sombre mood. Twice he tried to say something pleasant, and each time she nearly bit his head off. In the end he took himself off for a walk.

He wandered rather aimlessly along the path that led to the woods where they had seen the red squirrel, and when he came to a clearing on the shores of the creek he sat down on a fallen tree trunk. The water was calm this morning, its surface glassy as a mirror. He picked up the flattest stone he could find and sent it skimming, but he was out of practice and it fell with a loud plop only a short distance away, startling a small black-and-white bird into flight. Immediately the bushes behind him parted and an angry red face appeared.

"Oh, it's you again!" said Solo O'Rourke. "Might have known it. You seem to make a habit of wrecking my best pictures."

"Sorry," said James. "I didn't know you were there. Were you drawing something?"

"Aye, an oyster catcher. But he's gone now and I doubt he'll be back." The bushes closed again as Solo disappeared.

"Hey, just a minute! I wanted to ask you something…" James plunged into the bushes after him. He saw the old man hurrying along the path ahead with his sketchpad tucked under his arm and ran to catch him up. "It's about Gull Cottage, where we're staying…"

Solo stopped dead. "What about Gull Cottage?" he demanded.

"I was wondering … did that smuggler used to live there, the one who betrayed the gang? You know, Stew somebody."

"Stew Baker." Solo shot him a suspicious look from under bushy grey eyebrows. "Why do you ask?"

"It's just … well, the place has a strange atmosphere. I thought that if the gang came visiting with their axes … and that's where Stew Baker got murdered … it might explain why…" James couldn't finish the sentence.

The old man was looking too fierce.

"Who said he got murdered?" he demanded.

"I thought … you said they got their revenge."

"Aye, so they did, but not by killing Stew Baker. By the time they arrived he'd already done a runner, so they kidnapped his son instead."

"His son?"

"Nothing but a babe at the time. Naturally the mother gave chase, so it was her that got bumped off."

James stared at him. "What happened to the baby?"

"According to my grandsire one of the gang took it home and raised it as his own." Solo paused to blow his nose on a large, rather oily handkerchief. "Seems like his conscience got the better of him once the bloodlust had died down. Must have reckoned it was the least he could do, seeing as how the kid was left an orphan."

"But wasn't his father still alive?"

Solo shrugged. "Stew never came back.

The story goes he caught the first boat to America."

"How do you know all this?" James asked curiously. A sudden thought struck him. "Was it Silent O'Rourke who adopted the baby?"

"So the story goes."

"Then the baby must have been your grandfather?"

"My great-great-grandfather, more like!" Solo gave him a sideways look. "Why are you so interested?"

"Because it's history," James said evasively. "I like finding out about people who lived hundreds of years ago. Life was so much more exciting then than it is now."

"Depends what you mean by exciting. Meself, I could do with a bit more peace and quiet." The old man humped his shoulders and set off down the path.

James let him go. Solo had given him plenty to think about. Kezzie's nightmare, for a start. *Somebody coming into the house with the intention of taking the baby...* Perhaps Mum was wrong and Kezzie hadn't been dreaming after all. It was a good thing they had only one more night to go before the end of their holiday.

Chapter 14
The Ghost Woman

One more night before the end of the holiday!

Kezzie didn't think she could stand it. Nobody took her seriously when she said she wanted to go back to London straight away. Instead they kept telling her not to worry, she'd just had a bad dream and now it was daylight surely she could see how foolish she was being? But daylight made no difference as far as Kezzie was concerned.

Jan's attempts to be kind and understanding only made things worse. "Funny things crop up in our dreams," she said. "All sorts of unhappy memories from the past. But they will fade in time, Kezzie. You'll see."

In the end she was forced to take refuge in her room. "I hate this place!" she muttered under her breath; and she began to plot her escape.

Timing would be vital. If she left immediately after lunch and walked up to the village she could catch the bus and be well away from Jacob's Creek before anyone noticed she was missing. The only problem was money. All she had in her purse was seven pounds and a few odd coins. Still, that should be enough to cover the ferry fare and once she was safely on the train to London she could always tell the ticket collector that she had lost her ticket. If he turned nasty and handed her over to the police so what? She would far rather be locked up in a cell than spend another night in Gull Cottage.

"Kez?" James's voice came from outside on the landing. "Kezzie, are you there?"

"Go away," she mumbled.

The door opened and he peered in. "What are you doing?"

"Nothing. Leave me alone."

James hovered uncertainly in the doorway. He looked as if he wanted to say something but couldn't find the right words.

"Are you deaf?" Kezzie demanded. "I said *leave me alone!*"

He cleared his throat. "Mum sent me up to tell you to get ready. Dad's taking us to Alum Bay."

"You'll have to go without me. I'm staying here."

"No, Kezzie," said Jan, appearing behind James. "You're coming with us. It'll do you good to get out."

And in the end she had no choice but to go.

To her horror it turned out that Rob planned to make a day of it, which threatened to wreck her chances of escape. All through lunch in a clifftop café she sat silent, rethinking her plans; and she remained silent in the cable car ride down to the pebbly beach at Alum Bay, while the others oohed and aahed at the spectacular rainbow cliffs. She was silent in the Pleasure Park, and in the souvenir shop selling glass ornaments filled with coloured sand, and on the journey home.

The strange thing was that James seemed as preoccupied as she was. When they got back to Gull Cottage Jan asked, "Are you two all right? You've hardly said a word all day. I hope it wasn't something you ate?"

James muttered no, he felt fine. Kezzie said, "I feel a bit sick. I think maybe I'll go and lie down for a while," which was all part of her plan.

Upstairs in her room she began to get her things together. No luggage. That would slow her down and give her away if she was caught. Just her purse and a coat and a few personal things in her tote bag. It wasn't as if she would never see her clothes again: the others could bring them back in the car. The only practical problem might be getting into the Tollivers' house, but if necessary she would have to break a window and climb in. No one could accuse her of burglary because it was her home.

She left her room and stood on the landing,

listening. All she could hear was music. The others must be watching television. But she had only taken a couple of steps when Jan came out of the kitchen and called up the stairs, "Kezzie, do you want any supper?"

Kezzie pressed herself against the wall. "No, thanks."

"Sure?"

"Absolutely."

She went back into her room. Outside it was already getting dark, but this only made her more determined than ever to escape. With the darkness came danger … and she intended to be miles away before the ghostly riders paid their regular nightly visit. She waited until the others were settled in the sitting room, eating their supper off trays, then tried again.

The stairs creaked as she descended, but luckily the television was turned up loud, too loud for anyone to hear. Stealthily she crept through the hall and out of the front door, bending low on the path in case someone should spot her through the uncurtained window. Now she knew why it was so dark. Thunder clouds covered the sky and it had already begun to rain. She pulled up the hood of her anorak and hurried over the bridge, anxious to get as far away from Gull Cottage as possible before anyone noticed she had gone.

As she drew near the stricken oak something moved. Kezzie caught her breath, staring as a vague shape emerged from the hollow tree trunk and stood on the road in front of her.

The ghost woman!

There was no mistaking that pale face and wild dark hair. As to whether or not she had legs Kezzie didn't wait to find out. She turned and ran hard in the direction of the village until she got a stitch in her side and was forced to slow down. Even then she kept up a good pace, not daring to stop and look over her shoulder. The sooner she got away from this place the better!

By the time she reached the village she was rain-soaked and out of breath. She had no idea how often the buses ran, but with any luck one would come along soon. In the meantime she had no choice but to stand at the bus stop and wait. At least there was plenty of traffic about at this time of day, cars and vans with their headlights sweeping past her on the road. There was something reassuring about traffic. In a few more hours, Kezzie thought, she would be safely back in London.

In a few more hours...

The horrors would just be starting at Gull Cottage. The others had no idea of the danger they were in. They had refused to listen when she tried to warn them. They didn't know that the ghost woman lurked outside, watching and waiting...

And the Squaller – what would happen to him if the riders came again in the night, with their evil knocking and whispering? This time, without Kezzie to bar their way, they might manage to get inside Rob and Jan's room, to reach the cot where the baby was innocently sleeping...

Her mouth went dry and her legs felt weak with indecision.

At last the bus came came into sight with its windows lit and a load of cheerful-looking passengers. It drew to a halt and the doors opened, but Kezzie waved it on. She watched it disappear round the bend and then slowly, reluctantly, began to walk back down to the road to Jacob's Creek.

"I can't do it," she muttered to herself. "I can't run away and leave them to the ghosts. I'm the only one who knows what's going on."

All too soon she came within sight of Gull Cottage. Her footsteps began to falter. Why had she come back? She should have escaped when she had the chance. But then, as she crossed the bridge, she heard the Squaller begin to cry and knew she had no choice.

She had almost reached the front door when she felt a light tap on her shoulder. Startled, she swung round to see a dark form standing behind her. "Who is it?" she demanded, shielding her eyes from the rain. "What do you want?"

138

The ghost woman stepped forward into the light. "I've come for my baby," she said.

Kezzie screamed.

Chapter 15
The Jasper Test

"What was that?" asked Mum.

"Sounded like someone screaming," said Dad.

"I think it came from outside." James leaped to his feet and raced into the hall.

As he opened the front door Kezzie stumbled over the step, rainwater dripping from her clothes. "It's the ghost," she gasped. "She's come for her baby."

James, looking past her into the darkness, saw a woman standing hesitantly on the path. "Hello," he said. "Can I help you?"

Dad came out of the sitting room. "Kezzie, what on earth's the matter?"

"How did you get so wet?" asked Mum, close behind him.

James went on staring at the woman. Surely he had seen her somewhere before? She looked so strange with her hair hanging down in wisps, her dark eyes fixed pleadingly on his face. He remembered Kezzie's words as she stumbled into the house... *It's the ghost!*

"Who are you?" he asked, his voice little more than a croak. "What do you want?"

"My name's Dilys Jones." She started to cry. "And please I want my baby back."

Mum came forward, reaching out her hand. "You'd better come in out of the rain," she said.

The next half hour was very confused, with everyone talking at once and asking questions, and Dilys Jones weeping as she explained why she had left her newborn baby on the steps of St Brandon's Church. She had been ill, she said, and thought it would be for the best; but afterwards, when she felt better, she bitterly regretted giving him up and had tried to find out where he was living. It took her ages, and when she did finally track him down it was only to discover that his foster family had gone on holiday to the Isle of Wight. Their neighbours had given her this address, but when she found them her courage failed and she was filled with doubt. They seemed such a happy family. Perhaps her baby would be better off with them than with his real mother? For the past two days she had slept rough, just trying to catch a glimpse of her baby, and when she finally did she knew without a shadow of doubt that she wanted him back. At this point she began to weep again, and Mum wept too, and in all the commotion nobody seemed to notice how quiet Kezzie was keeping. Except James.

Later he found her alone in the kitchen, drinking a mug of tea. She had changed out of her wet clothes, but still shivered. James cleared his throat. "Kez, why did you think she was a ghost?"

Kezzie shrugged. "I've seen her around a few times and she didn't appear to have any legs, but I suppose that must have been the mist. Anyway, she looked pretty spooky."

He nodded. "I saw her too, when I was walking down to the quay. She did look odd, probably because she's dressed in rather old-fashioned clothes. But when you saw her this evening … what were you doing outside? Were you running away?"

"I meant to, but I only got as far as the bus stop."

"Why? Was it because you hate us?"

She shook her head. "It's this place I hate. I wanted to get away before … before tonight."

"Tonight?"

But she refused to say any more.

James sat down opposite. "If it makes you feel any better, I've heard things as well. You know, hoofbeats on the road outside … that sort of stuff."

She looked amazed. "Then why haven't you said anything?"

"For the same reason you haven't, I suppose. Because we didn't want people laughing at us."

Kezzie said slowly, "They come every

night. And I know why."

"So do I. I heard the story from Solo O'Rourke, the old guy we met who paints wildlife. His family have lived here for generations, so he knows all about the history of the creek. It was him that told me about the smugglers coming to take revenge on Stew Baker for betraying them."

"Oh, you and your history!" Kezzie said impatiently. "It's got nothing to do with smugglers. Gary Dent told me the real story. It's about a woman who got murdered here years ago."

"Yes, Stew Baker's wife! The gang couldn't find him so they took his baby and murdered his wife instead."

Kezzie stared at him. "Last night the riders came into the house, whispering up the stairs. I was trying to stop them getting to Brandon…" She stopped, then said jerkily, "That's why I came back, because I was afraid it might happen again tonight."

James swallowed hard. "We won't let it," he said. "We'll keep watch and make sure it doesn't. Meet me here, in the kitchen, eleven-thirty."

So much talking went on that evening it began to look as if no one had any intention of going to bed. But eventually Mum said, "I suggest we leave everything until we get back to London tomorrow. In the meantime, Dilys, I'll make you up a bed down here on the sofa."

James and Kezzie exchanged a look. "She can have my bed," Kezzie said quickly. "I'll sleep on the sofa."

After some argument Mum agreed, and by eleven-fifteen everyone had at last retired. James waited until he could hear Baz breathing evenly beneath his pillow, then pulled on his dressing-gown and crept downstairs. He found Kezzie in the kitchen, huddled in her anorak.

"I hope you're not planning to run away again?" he said.

"That's what Jan said. I told her wild horses wouldn't drag me out of this place tonight." Kezzie smiled grimly. "Or their riders."

They settled down to wait. Outside the wind howled and the rain beat against the window.

"I wonder what will happen," said James in a whisper. "I mean, about Dilys and the Squaller. It's funny, her following him all the way to the Island just to get a glimpse of him."

"Not really," said Kezzie. "Women are like that about babies. They get sort of demented if they lose them. I reckon that's the problem with the ghost. The real one, I mean. The ghost of the woman who used to live here."

"Stew Baker's wife."

"Us coming here with a baby must have disturbed her, and now she keeps reliving the night when they came to take hers away."

James nodded. "Over and over again, like a tape recorder. That's why when *our* baby cries it sets off the ghost baby, and then the whole performance starts, from the riders coming along the road and knocking on the door…"

"And coming upstairs to snatch the baby…"

"And then her following them on to the bridge." He hesitated. "Did you know she was drowned?"

Kezzie shivered. "I've seen her face in the water."

"So have I."

For a while they sat silent, listening to the wind and the beating rain.

Then James said, "What are we going to do? I mean … if we hear them coming, how are we going to stop them?"

"I don't know," Kezzie confessed. "Except … I don't think it's the riders we've got to stop. It's the ghost herself. We only hear the riders because *she* heard them, but if we could find some way to put her mind at rest…"

From upstairs came the sound of the Squaller crying. James groaned. "Oh, no!"

They heard Mum's voice, and then Dilys's, and after a while things seemed to go quiet. "It sounds as if Jan's given him to Dilys to look after," said Kezzie.

But almost at once the crying began again, this time more faintly. "That's not the Squaller," said Kezzie. "It must be the ghost baby. That means it's starting."

James shivered, suddenly cold. "You can feel it," he said. "You can feel the atmosphere changing. I was afraid the crying would upset her."

Kezzie looked tense. "Yes, well … you'd be upset if your kid was murdered."

"But he wasn't," said James, only half paying attention. Was that the sound of hoof-beats he had heard?

"What?" Kezzie's attention was also diverted. She glanced towards the door.

James tried to ignore what was happening outside. "I said he wasn't murdered. One of the gang took the baby home and brought him up as part of his own family. He was Solo O'Rourke's great-great-grandfather."

The hoofbeats were too loud to ignore any longer. They drew to a halt outside the cottage and then came the sound of knocking.

Kezzie stared at him. "But the ghost

doesn't know that, does she? If we could tell her it might stop the tape."

"How can we tell her? You can't talk to a ghost."

"We can try." White-faced, she leaped to her feet. "He wasn't murdered!" she shouted into the air. "Did you hear that? *He wasn't murdered!*"

The knocking stopped. There was a deep silence both inside and outside the cottage, as if Time was holding its breath. Even the wind seemed miraculously to have died and the rain no longer beat against the windows.

"He wasn't murdered," Kezzie repeated in a quieter voice. She no longer needed to shout to make herself heard. "Silent O'Rourke took him home and brought him up. James has met his grandson…"

"His great-great-grandson," James said.

"So you see, you don't have to worry any more." Kezzie faltered. Was she saying the right thing? She had never talked to a ghost before. How could she make it understand? She added firmly, "That means you can go now. There's no reason for you to stay here any longer. You can rest in peace."

There came a long, long sigh, like the slow letting out of a breath. Then the sound of the wind and the rain returned, but not so loudly, as if the storm was lessening. James and Kezzie stared at each other.

"I think we've done it," said Kezzie.

"*You* did it," said James. "It was you who realized what the ghost needed to know."

At that instant the kitchen door flew open. "What was all the shouting about?" demanded Dad. "I hope you two aren't fighting again?"

They burst out laughing, shaky with triumph and relief.

Next day Mrs Dent came to see them off. "I hope you enjoyed your holiday," she said, and they assured her they had. Baz bade a sad farewell to Jasper before climbing into the back of the car. Mum squeezed in beside him with Alison, while Dilys sat on the other side with the baby.

"Where's Kezzie?" asked Dad.

"She went to find Jasper," said Mrs Dent. "Said she wanted to do some kind of test."

Dad sighed. "If she doesn't hurry we'll miss the ferry."

A moment later Kezzie came flying across the bridge with Jasper on the lead. She handed him over to Mrs Dent with a muttered explanation and came to join them by the car. "I wanted to make sure," she told James in a low voice. "That's why I took Jasper on to the bridge. But it was OK! He didn't turn a hair."

"What did you just say to Mrs Dent?" James asked.

"Oh, I told her not to worry, we've put her ghost to rest so she'll be able to let the cottage to lots of people from now on. Actually she looked pretty gobsmacked."

"I'm not surprised," said James with a grin.

"Come on, you two," urged Dad. "Get into the car."

"I'll go in the back," James said quickly. "Kezzie can sit in the front with you and navigate."

Dad looked surprised, but didn't argue. Kezzie looked pleased.

"That was nice of you," Mum whispered as James squashed in beside her. Under cover of the engine she added, "I've had an idea. If Brandon goes back to Dilys we shall have a vacancy, so to speak, so I thought I might try to find out what happened to Kezzie's younger brothers and sisters. What do you think?"

"Mum," said James nervously, "you do realize that Kezzie had *four* brothers and sisters?"

"Ssssh! Don't let her hear, because it may not be possible. But there's no harm in making enquiries."

James groaned.